Picking th

Jade Winters

Picking the Right Heart

by Jade Winters

Published by Wicked Winters Books

Copyright © 2017 Jade Winters

www.jade-winters.com

ISBN: 978-1-979-20267-1

Other titles by Jade Winters

Standalone Novels

143
Caught By Love
Guilty Hearts
Say Something
Faking It
Second Thoughts
Secrets
In It Together
Love Interrupted
The Song, The Heart
Accidentally Together
Flirting With Danger
Lost In You
Just One Destiny
Unravelled
Starting Over Again

The Ashley McCoy Detective Series

A Walk Into Darkness
Everything To Lose

Novellas

Talk Me Down From The Edge

Chapter One

Adriana gritted her teeth. Nothing annoyed her more than having her knickers halfway down her legs, and someone attempting to force the lavatory door open. As was happening right now. The thin plywood door rattled in its frame, this was then followed by urgent tap, tap, taps in quick succession. To anyone with common sense, a locked door meant the toilet was either occupied or out of use. Adriana exhaled in relief, thankful she was just about finished, and flushed the chain. Sliding the lock across, she mentally geared herself up to give the eager beaver outside a piece of her mind.

'Can't you see it's —'

Her rehearsed speech was cut short when the door was forcefully pushed open, and a pair of perfectly manicured fingers thrust her backwards, causing her to lose her balance and fall into a sitting position on the toilet seat with a thud.

Wedged tightly between the cistern and the intruder, Adriana shrieked, 'Claudia what are you—'

Before she could utter another word, Claudia was upon her, lips and tongue pressing outside and inside of her mouth. Her frantic hands swept over Adriana's chest and abdomen like a police officer frisking a criminal. Any attempt to extricate herself only resulted in Claudia pushing back hard, pinning Adriana's arms either side of her.

Not only was it incredibly uncomfortable, there was zero sexiness about being mauled on a public toilet seat by a woman she'd shared a drunken snog with a couple of weeks earlier.

When Claudia's hand slipped inside Adriana's silk shirt and attempted to tweak her nipple between her finger and thumb as if she were honking a horn, Adriana decided enough was enough. With an almighty heave, she pushed up, becoming breathless as she forced Claudia's body weight off her.

Claudia fell into a runner's stance, ready to pounce again.

'If you don't get out of my way, I'm going to scream,' Adriana said more out of annoyance than fear.

Claudia ran her tongue across her lips, which were now smudged with red lipstick, making her mouth resemble that of a clown. 'Don't be so melodramatic, we're only having a bit of fun, darling.'

'Fun?' Adriana said tersely. 'Do I look like I'm having fun?'

Claudia took a step towards her and Adriana held up her hand in mid-air. 'Stop right there.'

'Or what?' Claudia eyed her so sceptically that Adriana knew there was only one way to make her see sense.

Adriana took a deep breath, closed her eyes and opened her mouth. The scream, when she released it, was so piercing Claudia covered her ears with both hands.

'All right, all right,' a wide-eyed Claudia shouted in

order to make herself heard.

Adriana clamped her mouth shut, and with a wag of her finger indicated for Claudia to step aside, which she begrudgingly did. Adriana pulled the door open, stepped outside the cubicle, then turned back to Claudia. 'That's no way to treat a lady ... darling.'

Adriana crossed over to the basin, washed her hands then with her head held high, as if it would give her more dignity, made her way back into Le Sacre Coeur's jovial atmosphere.

Once seated at her table, Adriana shook off her irritation with Claudia and resumed entertaining her friends with shenanigans from her latest trip to Peru. All the while waiters, in one of London's most expensive French restaurants, served lobster, crab and oysters by the dozen, all washed down with chilled bottles of Dom Perignon.

Adriana didn't believe in doing things by half when it came to dinner parties. The bill for the evening would probably be in the region of £3,000, but who cared? At twenty-two, Adriana was the only granddaughter of the wealthy Beatrice Colfield, and apart from the very generous monthly allowance she received, Adriana had several bank cards linked to Beatrice's account. Which meant she had the means to treat her friends to lavish dinner parties every evening if she wished.

'Can I bring you another bottle of champagne, madame?' the waiter asked as Adriana slurped down an oyster.

'Enzo, I think you'd better make it two, my friends

are thirsty by the looks of things.'

'At this rate they won't have any champagne left, Addy,' Imogen, her childhood friend announced cheerfully, raising her glass in appreciation.

Adriana and Imogen had been friends since boarding school, and they still remained close, seeing each other weekly, despite Imogen recently becoming second in command of her father's multi-million pound textile company.

Soon Enzo was back with two bottles of champagne, and Adriana rose to her feet to address the table. 'A toast. To the good times and an eternal fountain of champagne!'

With that, Adriana swooped down and theatrically kissed Anne, the cute blonde woman seated next to her, full on the lips. Her friends gave a heartfelt round of applause, all except Claudia, who shot her a killer look before abruptly turning away to talk to Maxi and Penelope. Adriana thought it rude and unbecoming for Claudia to be upset with her because she had rejected her advances. Not to mention it being very disrespectful to hit on her when she knew Anne, Adriana's date for the night, was sitting outside.

'You are so fucking hot. I can't wait to get you alone,' Anne whispered in Adriana's ear when she sat down. Anne shifted closer and discreetly slid her hand between Adriana's warm thighs.

Heat crept into Adriana's cheeks and her erect nipples strained against the lace material of her bra. Adriana's eyes searched from left to right, double checking that no one could tell where Anne's hand was, but Maxi's eagle eye had noticed something was amiss.

'Hey, you two, cool your jets. There'll be plenty of time for bedroom gymnastics later.' Maxi playfully threw a piece of bread at Adriana.

'Food fight!' Penelope shouted as if they were once again kids at boarding school. Soon there were pieces of bread flying across the table in every direction.

It didn't take long for Enzo to appear at Adriana's side, speaking in a low diplomatic voice. 'I'm sorry to disturb you, madame, but some of the other diners are complaining about the … ahem … behaviour of the guests at your table.'

'Please give my sincerest apologies and a glass of champagne to each guest for any inconvenience caused,' Adriana said, slipping Enzo a fifty-pound note.

Enzo gave a slight bow. 'Thank you, madame, that's very generous of you.'

'It's the least I can do,' Adriana said before asking her friends to tone their banter down a couple of notches.

Enzo thanked her for being so understanding and slipped the money into his trouser pocket before retreating.

Adriana sipped her champagne while people watching in the crowded room. She couldn't help but notice how the glamorous women dripped in diamonds and the men, though less obvious in showcasing their wealth, still managed to expose their Rolex watches when their sleeves rode up their arm every time they knocked back an expensive glass of wine.

Adriana smiled wryly to herself. It was a world she felt comfortable in. After all, she too came from money and she was a firm believer that the only way to enjoy it was to spend it. And spend it she did, with the complete blessing of her grandmother. Beatrice was the true matriarch of her family as she'd inherited all of her husband's wealth after he'd passed away fifteen years ago. Though Beatrice still kept a very firm grip on family matters and liked to know what was coming in and out of her account, that didn't mean she wasn't generous to a fault. Because she was, not only with money, but love and affection as well. Adriana adored Beatrice from the tips of her toes, to the ends of her long silky grey hair that Adriana loved to brush tenderly, even now as an adult. Sometimes if the truth be known, Adriana thought she actually loved Beatrice more than she did her own mother.

No matter what your circumstances, always remember to stop and smell the flowers along the way, Beatrice would remind Adriana when she was flapping around like a headless chicken, trying to get a million things done at once. And she also encouraged Adriana to enjoy her life one day at a time. Not to dream about how happy she was going to be *some day* in the future, but to live in the now.

Today is the only day we've got, so live it like it's your last, was another of Beatrice's expressions, and Adriana memorised every word as if they were her own thoughts.

Adriana's parents often remarked that Adriana had Beatrice's heart beating in her chest, and that's why she was such an adventurous woman.

Growing up, Adriana's favourite activities had been rock climbing, scuba diving and sailing; that was until she was taken skiing for her fifteenth birthday. Ever since then, skiing had become somewhat of an obsession for her, and she had finally managed to persuade Beatrice to buy a ski lodge in the Swiss Alps. Although Adriana had wanted to live there permanently and become a ski instructor, she didn't want to leave her eighty-year-old grandmother, so she had put the idea on the back burner and stayed in London, only getting away to ski over the holidays. The rest of the time, Adriana helped run the family's investment accounts, which didn't take up too much of her time and left her with ample opportunity to hang out at glitzy restaurants and nightclubs in London.

The rowdy dinner party might well have carried on into the early hours of the morning, was it not for the fact that the restaurant had a strict policy of closing at midnight.

'Thanks for a great night,' echoed around the table before her friends got up and left, talking animatedly amongst themselves as they exited the building. All who remained were Anne and Imogen who were still sipping their drinks.

Enzo appeared at Adriana's side and presented her with the bill.

'Add a twenty percent tip for yourself,' Adriana

said, placing her credit card on the silver tray.

Enzo's eyes widened. 'Are you sure, madame? That will be a tip of just over £600!'

'Mmm, you're right, I *am* being a bit stingy … make it £700. You've looked after us well this evening, Enzo,' Adriana said with a wink.

'In that case, thank you very much.' Still grinning from ear to ear, Enzo slotted her credit card in the card machine and handed it to her for her to type in the pin number.

'I love a generous woman,' Anne said, snuggling up against her.

Adriana absent-mindedly tapped the keypad while her eyes glanced furtively at Anne's exposed cleavage. She couldn't wait to get her home and get her hands on those.

'I'm sorry, madame, but there seems to be a problem. I'm sure it's just a technical glitch, but your card has been declined,' Enzo said quietly and handed her back her Platinum credit card. Adriana frowned slightly but took it in her stride and pulled another card out of her purse.

'Try this one, and add another £100 for your trouble.' Adriana gave what she hoped was a reassuring smile at a perturbed Anne.

'I'm sorry … I really don't know what's going on, but this card has also been declined,' Enzo said a minute later.

Adriana looked up in genuine surprise, but now there was a real note of concern in her voice as she handed Enzo yet another card. Enzo repeated the process only to shake his head again.

'This one has also been declined.'

'You know, baby, I'm feeling tired,' Anne said, slipping into her jacket. 'I think I'll catch a taxi home. I'll see you around.'

Adriana was so flummoxed she was speechless. All she could do was watch in total incomprehension as Anne hurried towards the exit and soon disappeared.

'What a bitch, running off at the first sign of trouble,' Imogen said with a shake of her head.

'She's the least of my worries.' Adriana frantically searched her purse for another card. What the hell was going on? She couldn't have spent that much money already, it was only the first week of the month.

Imogen in the meantime had handed Enzo her credit card. 'Here, use mine.'

Enzo nodded gratefully and inserted Imogen's card into the machine, and within seconds, his face broke out into a smile.

'Thank you, madame, your card has been accepted, and the bill has been paid.'

'Thanks, Imogen. I really don't know what's going on,' Adriana said as they walked out of the restaurant side by side.

'Seems your grandma finally woke up to your ways and cut you off,' Imogen joked, but Adriana felt panic flash through her mind as she wondered if Imogen could be right.

Adriana glanced at her watch after seeing off

Imogen in a taxi and saw that it was just past midnight. She knew her parents were going to be annoyed with her, but she simply needed to know what was going on. Adriana fished her phone out of her bag and turned it off silent. Before she had time to dial her mother's number, she saw that there were ten missed calls from her.

Seeing this made her slightly nervous. *It can't be that bad, she would have left a message if anything.* Trying to reassure herself all was well, Adriana dialled her mum's number, as she knew that her dad would never be awake at this hour.

Alice always answered her phone, no matter what time it was. She picked up straight away.

'Hi, Mum. Sorry to phone so late, but all of my bank cards were declined at a restaurant tonight. I was just wondering what's going on?'

'Adriana, I was trying to get hold of you earlier.' Alice gave a muffled cry.

Adriana's head tingled, and her fingers trembled as she gripped the phone tighter. 'Is Dad—'

'It's not your dad, it's … your granny. She passed away.'

'Oh, no … Mum don't say that. Please, no.'

Adriana sank to her knees beside her car. Tears spilt down her cheeks. The news of her granny's passing was a big blow to her, and suddenly Adriana wished she would have spent the day with her instead of rushing off after lunch, thinking she would see her the following day. *That we had time.*

Guilt overwhelmed Adriana knowing that she could have been there with Beatrice. Held her hand and told her how much she loved her. *Just to have one more second to say goodbye.*

'She didn't suffer, darling. The doctor said she wouldn't have felt a thing, she just … fell asleep ….' the sound of her mother's voice floated up from where Adriana had dropped the phone on the floor.

Adriana picked the phone up and pressed it to her ear. 'Where is … she now.' She could barely get the words past the lump in her throat.

'The undertakers—'

'I don't want to hear anymore,' Adriana sobbed. She didn't want to imagine Beatrice's body anywhere but at her ridiculously elegant penthouse apartment, which was filled with crystals and pendants Beatrice believed had special energies.

'I'm sorry, darling, but don't worry about your credit cards; the entire estate has been frozen until the solicitors can sort out all of the financial stuff in the morning.'

'I don't give a damn about my credit cards or anything else, I just want … *my granny back.* I've got to go. I'll see you tomorrow … And Mum?'

'Yes, darling?'

'I'm … I'm so sorry for your loss.' Adriana disconnected the call before her mother could reply.

Climbing into her car, Adriana rested her forehead on the steering wheel, her heart in her mouth as she pictured the day Beatrice had presented her with the

Ferrari she was now sat in. Although Adriana had been thrilled with her present, it wasn't the car that had made it such a joyous occasion. It was seeing the expression on Beatrice's face, which had been one of bliss. Her laughter had been contagious as they belted up and whizzed around London. It had truly been one of the best days of Adriana's life.

Leaning back, she pulled up a photo of Beatrice on her phone. She had taken it on her 80th birthday four months previously and it was Adriana's favourite and most treasured by far. Beatrice's eyes sparkled back at her, her smile wide. Adriana remembered the day as if it were yesterday. As a birthday treat, she had taken Beatrice to a new Spanish restaurant that had just opened on the King's Road in Chelsea, and Beatrice had been delighted with each of the spicy tapas dishes she ate. Beatrice had even gone as far as saying she was glad she had lived long enough to experience it. Thinking about that statement now, Adriana couldn't help but wonder if Beatrice had somehow known her days were numbered.

Her vision blurred with tears, Adriana realised that she'd just lost the most important person in her life. *Rest in peace, Granny.*

Adriana felt the warmth and love from Beatrice's gaze seep into her soul as she kissed her picture. A final farewell.

'I know you're walking through the countryside somewhere,' Adriana whispered. 'Just remember to stop and smell the flowers along the way.'

Chapter Two

How bad can it really be? Jessica asked herself as she tucked the tail of her shirt into the waistband of her jeans. After all, her mum had told her a zillion times that her nan was a burlesque dancer back in her day and stripping was just an advanced form of burlesque. Wasn't it? Well that's what she'd been trying to convince herself of anyway. That she could somehow take her clothes off in front of a crowd of men and still be able to look herself in the mirror without feeling a sense of shame. *I'd be selling my soul to the devil for money*, a critical voice quipped out of nowhere.

But what choice did she have? Stay at her job waitressing for peanuts and be broke for the rest of her life, or do the only other alternative, which was to apply for a job at the Sleazy Slum. A club where, according to the women who worked there, the dancers-come-strippers could earn up to £200 a night in tips alone. The difference that sort of money would make in her life would be astronomical, as it was four times the amount she earned by slogging her guts out at The Fry Up.

It wasn't all about the money of course. There were a multitude of reasons why she needed a change of career. For starters, Jessica had reached the end of her tether with the obnoxious customers who were rude to her for no other reason than they could be. Not to mention the annoying ones who sent their food back to be reheated when it wasn't exactly the right temperature for their connoisseur tastes. This normally happened bang in the middle of the cafe's busiest times. And what really, really pissed her off the most, was having to put up with horny old men who thought it was acceptable to grab her arse every time she turned her back on them.

If Jessica had to endure that crap, she might as well get paid for it.

Biting on her bottom lip, Jessica eyed herself critically in the full-length mirror hanging on the wall, and gave serious thought as to whether or not she was attractive enough to compete with the other women.

Her long blonde hair, which normally couldn't decide if it wanted to be straight, frizzy or curly, wasn't a problem today because she'd swept it back into a ponytail which served to accentuate her green eyes and high cheek bones. *Hmm, suppose my face isn't that bad.* Next, she gave her body the once over; Five foot eight, toned and slender—*yes,* Jessica decided, she could easily give the women over at the Sleazy Slum a run for their money.

'And you two aren't half bad either.' Jessica smiled to herself as she looked down at her 36D breasts and jiggled them the way a stripper might do.

Clipping her name tag on her shirt, Jessica walked out of the staff room and into the spacious cafe with its familiar aroma of cooking oil.

'Hey, Jess,' Keith, the chef shouted from the kitchen the second she showed her face. 'Two orders for table six!'

Keith, a balding man in his fifties, had left his wife and three kids to move from Ireland to the UK so he could follow his dreams of becoming a celebrity chef. But when reality hit home, and he realised that he actually needed imagination and the ability to fry something more substantial than burgers and eggs, he ended up working at The Fry Up rather than returning home with his tail between his legs to a wife that no longer wanted him.

'I'm on it,' Jessica shouted back, and soon she was running and dancing between tables, not even stopping to take a breather.

'You look like you're in good form, lovey. No one's managed to get their hands on your arse yet,' Ariel, her co-worker, said in a heavy northern accent.

'Give it time,' Jessica replied. She looked over at Ariel's gorgeous face; big brown eyes and a generous spread of freckles topped off with a mop of thick tight curls, and found herself wondering how someone with her appeal hadn't been snatched up by a sexy hot woman yet. Ariel had once confided in Jessica that she had fallen in love with a woman once but things were too complicated for them to be together.

Ben, the cafe's owner, came up behind them. 'Hey, I don't pay the two of you to stand there twittering like love birds. Go serve some food.'

Jessica opened her mouth to give a rude retort but stopped herself just in time. *Now's not the time to get on the wrong side of him.* Instead she replied sweetly, 'Just remember what you said, Ben. Next Friday, we're gonna discuss my pay rise, right?'

As Jessica strode away to clear the tables, Ben called after her, 'If standing around yapping is your way of trying to convince me to give you a rise, you're going to have to up your game, missy.'

'Whatever,' Jessica muttered under her breath as she scooped up the empty plates and piled them on top of one another.

The rest of the evening went off without incident, apart from when Jessica 'accidently' knocked over a cup of warm coffee onto a customer's lap. Jessica had to admit she enjoyed seeing the pained expression on his face as the liquid made contact with his private parts. He'd been especially rude and demanding, and she was so tempted to tell him that he deserved it, and would have done had Ben not been standing nearby. Her boss wasn't pleased about the incident and had cornered her, saying in a quiet steely tone that the chance of her getting a rise was dwindling by the second.

The more I think about it, the more I'd like to tell Ben to take a running jump, Jessica told herself as she walked home through the quiet streets of Hackney. Unlike herself, the dancers at Sleazy Slum could actually afford a taxi home. *And they can also afford to live in a decent area, not one of the poorest boroughs in London.*

Reaching home, Jessica closed the door behind her to the studio flat she rented and found herself drowning even further in pity. Never mind work or all the other crappy things that constituted her life at the moment.

How long had it actually been since she'd had a potential lover over for dinner or drinks at her place? *Too long!* The more Jessica thought about it, the more she realised her entire life seemed to centre around her shifts at the cafe. And in the meantime, she wasn't getting younger, *or getting any sex.* All right, so she was only twenty-three, but time flew and Jessica didn't want to end up like one of those 40-year-old spinsters surrounded by a zillion cats and Netflix as her only companions.

Dropping her rucksack on the floor in the narrow hallway, Jessica stepped into the bathroom that was so cold she was surprised icicles weren't dangling from the ceiling. Bending over the bath to turn on the tap, Jessica was shocked by how exhausted she felt just by doing such a small everyday action. The only thing she could put her tiredness down to was the unsociable hours at the cafe. All work and no play was not only making Jessica very dull, it was literally draining the life out of her.

And right about now she needed to be mentally strong to make a decision one way or the other.

Obviously Jessica hoped Ben would come through on his promise, and give her the extra bit of money she needed to top up her wage. But sadly, knowing Ben the way she did, it was a shot in the dark.

Life sucks when you're poor.

Chapter Three

Although the initial problem with Beatrice's finances had been sorted out, it appeared that Adriana's monthly allowance had been cut off until further notice. Unbeknown to Adriana, the arrangement was only meant to last for as long as Beatrice was alive. But Adriana's lack of money hadn't mattered to her in the end. The last thing she wanted was to socialise and have fun. For now, she was content with spending her evenings alone, reflecting on her life now that Beatrice was no longer in it.

Although Beatrice's funeral had been a sombre occasion, Adriana had been thankful for the opportunity to meet so many of Beatrice's friends. Each and every one of them had stories to tell of Beatrice's acts of kindness. By the end of the day, a sense of peace enveloped Adriana and that feeling had stayed with her. Whereas before, Adriana would cry thinking of Beatrice, she now smiled, grateful to have so many more wonderful memories to add to her own. Even now, as she waited in Mr Griffin's wood panelled office, Adriana could feel her presence.

The bespectacled solicitor cleared his throat, fussing with sheets of paper as he readied himself to read Beatrice's will. Adriana sat quietly, her parents either side of her, while her Aunt Blossom sat directly behind them, letting out the occasional sniff and sob, for whose benefit Adriana didn't know.

She wasn't anywhere to be seen when Granny was alive. So I don't know why she's pretending she cares now. Only deep down, Adriana did know. Blossom was there to hear what Beatrice had left her, and Adriana was in no doubt that once Blossom got what she wanted, she'd be gone, never to be seen again until some other poorly relative died. Then like the vulture she was, she'd be back to pick over the bones.

Adriana tugged at the cuff of her black suit jacket which now swamped her slender frame. She had lost at least a stone in weight since Beatrice's death as the only calories she had been consuming were the ones she found at the bottom of a wine bottle. It wasn't quite the champagne she was used to, but alcohol was alcohol.

Anne had been calling her nonstop, but Adriana had simply ignored her and in the end, blocked her completely. It wasn't that Adriana was angry with her; she was simply shocked to discover how quickly Anne had abandoned her when it appeared she had a cash flow problem. Up until now, Adriana had never really given much thought to the loyalty of the people who surrounded her. But the incident at the restaurant had forced her to think about it, and she didn't like the idea of only being good enough for Anne when paying for her fun and entertainment.

'If we are all ready, I will commence with the reading of the will,' Mr Griffin said with quiet authority before running through Beatrice's will. The bulk of her estate was divided equally between a number of animal charities, and her penthouse apartment, paintings and jewellery were left between her surviving children Alice and Blossom. The only real quirk was the specific provision set out for Adriana.

'To my dearest beloved granddaughter Adriana, who was the joy of my life, I leave the sum of three million pounds.'

There was a loud gasp behind her, followed by low angry mutterings.

Three million pounds! Adriana felt light-headed.

'On the condition that she personally finds my long-lost friend Edwina Wilson, without the aid of a private detective, and hand-delivers to her the sealed letter which I append to this last will and testament. Only upon delivery to my solicitor of this letter with Edwina Wilson's authentic signature on it, or of a certificate indicating that Edwina is no longer alive, will the entire sum of three million pounds be released to Adriana.'

Adriana was slightly taken aback but she wasn't upset when the surprise clause outlining the condition for her generous inheritance was read out. In fact, she smiled as she thought how her beloved grandmother had planned one last adventure for the two of them together. Even if it meant Beatrice could only smile from the sky above at Adriana's efforts to locate her long-lost friend Edwina Wilson. *Whoever she is.*

Alice's eyes welled with tears as she smiled at Adriana. 'Granny thought the world of you.'

'I felt the same way about her,' Adriana said, squeezing Alice's hand, as her father weighed in on the conversation.

'Don't worry about money, we'll give you some to tide you over until you locate this mysterious woman—'

'Or, until you discover that she's already passed away,' Alice cut in, using her free hand to dab tissue at the corner of her eyes.

'Thank you, both of you. I really appreciate it,' Adriana said.

It wasn't that Adriana needed money as she wasn't exactly 'poor'. Her Chelsea apartment and Ferrari were fully paid off and registered in her name. The problem was that because of her free and easy spending habits, she didn't have any savings in the bank. So until she found Edwina Wilson, she would have to rein things in.

Even though Alice had brought up the suggestion that Edwina might have already passed away, Adriana didn't believe it for a single second. Something in her gut told her that Edwina was still very much alive and just waiting for Beatrice's letter to be delivered to her.

Later that evening, wine in hand, Adriana sat on her bed with her laptop resting on her lap and began looking for clues as to the whereabouts of Edwina Wilson. She assumed Edwina was around her grandmother's age, and at eighty probably didn't frequent social media sites such as Facebook, but she started there anyway.

No luck.

So Adriana googled 'Edwina Wilson' and soon realised that this was not going to get her anywhere either, as there were scores of people with Edwina's name and they all lived in different countries right across the globe. Added to that, there weren't any personal contact details written next to their search results in Google either. And even if there had been, it would take weeks to call or write to all of them. And Adriana didn't have weeks.

No matter what search function Adriana tried, she got nowhere and soon realised that she was going to have to take a more hands-on approach rather than simply finding Edwina's whereabouts on the internet.

Adriana wondered why Beatrice hadn't hired a private detective to track Edwina down herself. Was there something confidential about her past with Edwina which Beatrice only trusted Adriana to deal with?

Whatever the reason, Adriana now surmised that her search was not going to be something which she would be able to take care of without literally throwing all of her energy into.

And she would do it willingly. Not for the money, but because it was her grandmother's last wish. Though the urge to take a peek at the letter was strong Adriana resisted. If Beatrice had wanted her to know what was in the letter she would have told Adriana herself.

'Where on earth are you, Edwina?' Adriana said out loud as she closed her laptop.

She put her glass on the side and flopped back on her bed, letting her mind wander. Perhaps a sudden inspiration would come to her out of the blue and throw up the answer she needed. But seconds turned to minutes and there was nothing as Adriana drifted off to sleep and found herself in the midst of a very strange dream. She was standing in an airport arrivals lounge, holding up a sign that read 'Edwina Wilson'. In the dream, she was waiting for the mysterious woman to arrive after a long flight. Finally, a woman came walking in her direction, but her face was hidden behind a veil. When she came to a stop in front of Adriana, she slowly pulled away the veil, and Adriana was shocked to see the woman in front of her was not old at all, but a beautiful young girl with long red hair.

Adriana woke up with a jolt, wondering what the strange dream could have meant, but finally decided that it was probably her over-active imagination, and there wasn't a specific meaning. Deciding to carry on looking tomorrow, she undressed and slid naked beneath the covers. When Adriana closed her eyes, she hoped Beatrice would come to her in her dreams and let her know that she was okay. But when she finally fell asleep, the only person she dreamt of was Edwina Wilson.

***

The following morning, Adriana relaxed on her padded window seat, absent-mindedly staring out at the park opposite where a couple jogged off into the distance and an old man shuffled along with a Yorkshire terrier by his side. On a park bench directly underneath a weeping willow tree, she noticed a young woman reading a book. Adriana thought it must have been something engaging as the woman didn't look up once. Suddenly, a memory snapped into her mind. *Of course!* She'd forgotten one very important thing about her grandmother which could prove to be pivotal in her search. Beatrice used to have several diaries! And if they were still in her apartment, Adriana hazarded a guess they would be in her storage room where she kept her personal belongings.

Adriana sprang to her feet and rushed to her bedroom to get changed into a pair of jeans and a cashmere top. Minutes later, on her way out to her car, she called Alice to ask her if she could pick up the keys to Beatrice's apartment to search for her diaries.

'Yes, but you will have to hurry as your aunt Blossom already has the cleaners in. The estate agent put it up for sale today,' Alice said.

Adriana paused at her car door. 'You're selling it?! But Gran loved that apartment, Mum. You can't sell it, you just can't.'

The thought of someone else living in Beatrice's apartment mortified her. Beatrice would turn in her grave if she knew the fate of her home, the place she had loved and cherished for the past forty years.

'If it was just me, you know I wouldn't part with it. Blossom is adamant that we sell it. So it's out of my hands I'm afraid.'

Well it's not out of mine! Adriana said a quick goodbye before ending the call.

There was no way on earth that she was going to let Beatrice's apartment be sold. Even if it meant her buying the apartment herself. A quick look on Rightmove told her it was up for sale for a cool three million. The same amount she would be getting from her inheritance.

Adriana didn't even think twice about it. In her heart, she knew she had to buy it.

But first she had to find Edwina and fast.

Adriana jumped into her Ferrari and with the tyres screeching as she made off towards Kensington, she hoped she would get there before the cleaners threw Beatrice's diaries away.

Chapter Four

With a spring in her step, Jessica pushed open the door to The Fry Up and headed straight for Ben's office. It was Friday, and the showdown for her pay rise had arrived.

'Jessica,' Ben said as she opened his door. 'Sit down.'

The fact that he remembered their talk was taking place today had to be a good sign. Encouraged by this, the tension released in her shoulders as she sat opposite Ben. She would keep her mouth shut and let him lead the way.

'As you know, this place is going through a bit of a staff shortage. I just wanted to say that I truly appreciate the effort you've put in, especially all of the late shifts you've been working.'

'I'm glad to hear it.' Jessica was happy that her efforts had been recognised. 'I'm prepared to put in the hard work as long as there's some kind of financial reward at the end of it all.'

Ben shifted uncomfortably in his seat. 'Well … like I said, we're going through a bit of a tough time, and even though I appreciate the effort you've been making, I just can't afford to give you a pay rise at this time.'

Jessica gave him one of her sweetest smiles. Ben, in response, eyed her suspiciously.

She knew this wasn't what he had expected, that he had prepared himself for some kind of outburst.

'You know that staff shortage you're talking about?' Jessica asked still with the smile on her face.

'Yes?' Ben replied carefully.

'It just got fucking worse, 'cause I quit!' Jessica was on her feet in seconds and heading for the door.

'Jessica, wait a minute! In another two weeks or so we can take a look at the situation again!'

Jessica's response was to slam the door behind her with full force.

This was all she needed to help make a decision about her career. It was obvious her future lay at the Sleazy Slum. Her time here was done.

The Sleazy Slum was within walking distance of the cafe, and Jessica strode resolutely towards it, not wanting to give herself the chance to second guess her decision and change her mind.

'You're late, baby, the guys are going to be here en masse soon,' the burly bouncer at the door said when Jessica neared the entrance.

'What do you mean?' Jessica asked in confusion.

'You're here to dance, right?' the bouncer asked, looking as puzzled as she was.

'No, I just came to see your boss about a job,' she said, pointing at the 'Dancers wanted' ad in the window.

'Oh, in that case, go right in. Micky's office is down the hall and up the flight of stairs. It's the door on the right,' the bouncer said blatantly eyeing the outline of her chest.

Creep! Jessica followed his instructions, and after climbing up what she counted to be twenty steps, she stood outside a badly painted black door with the word manager scrawled on it in white paint. *Classy.*

'Come in!' a deep voiced boomed from behind the door.

After inhaling a mouthful of stale air, Jessica slowly exhaled as she pressed the door handle down and pushed it open.

'Helloooo, baby; you look mighty fine in them jeans, and you'll look even better when you take them off,' a man with a comb over and leery grin said. It was obviously a well-rehearsed line but that didn't make it sound any less corny.

Jessica slightly recoiled when he licked his heavily perspiring lips. *Oh, fuck, I can't back out now. I can't.*

The man introduced himself as Micky, and when he held out his hand, Jessica thought about ignoring it but quickly decided that would probably be a bad move. She needed this job, and didn't want to get off on the wrong foot with the owner.

Trying her hardest not to grimace, Jessica shook his hand. Her stomach turned over when she felt how clammy it was, and prayed to God it was only sweat. She made a quick mental note to thoroughly scrub her hands as soon as she got home.

Micky gestured for her to take a seat, and Jessica did so, keeping her head held high in the hope of coming across as confident when she felt nothing but deflated that her life had come to this. The universe seemed intent on shitting on her from a very great height lately.

'Talk,' Micky said, dangling a lit cigarette between his lips.

'Oh, okay,' Jessica said, momentarily caught off guard from watching the grey swirling smoke from his cigarette delicately float above his head. 'Well, I saw your ad for dancers in the window—'

'And you think you can cut it?' He inhaled deeply on his cigarette, holding the smoke in then releasing one perfectly formed ring at a time.

'Think?' Jessica said defensively. 'I know I can.'

'Prove it.'

Jessica raised her eyebrows. 'Prove it?'

'Dance for me now.' He leant back in his seat and let his gaze shamelessly roam from her face to her chest. 'Think of it as a live audition.'

Leave now, go, go, go! Her mind screamed, but her mouth opened, and she was shocked to hear herself saying, 'Fine.'

Ten minutes later, Jessica stood behind a red curtain which separated the dancers' dressing room from the stage. Beyoncé's 'Crazy in Love' suddenly blared from the speakers and Jessica couldn't help swaying her hips to the funky beat. All those years as a gymnast had prepared her for this moment, and she strode out on stage as if she was Beyoncé herself. Catching a glimpse of her body in the stage mirror as she made her way to the pole, Jessica had to admit she did look rather sexy in the silver bikini and cowboy hat

Micky had given her to wear.

A group of men milling around by the bar wolf-whistled at her as she placed her hands on the cool, chrome pole. Within seconds she was energetically moving up and down it like a true professional, blanking out her seedy surroundings as if she was in the room alone.

Jessica couldn't believe it when the music stopped, and she found herself feeling a sense of disappointment. Pole dancing had actually been like a vigorous work out.

'That was fucking great!' Micky called out as he neared the stage. 'Would've been even better if you'd have got your kit off.'

'My clothes come off when I get paid,' Jessica said breathlessly.

'Business savvy, eh?' Micky grinned. 'I like it.'

'So have I got the job?' Jessica asked, hoping her over-confident attitude hadn't pissed him off.

'Yeah, why not? You can start next Monday. It's a slow day, but you can ease yourself in and be ready for the weekend.'

'Great!' Jessica tried to inject enthusiasm into her voice, but it came out flat.

Micky didn't seem at all bothered. He just turned, and without so much as a goodbye, walked towards the exit and disappeared through the door.

Arriving home an hour later, the euphoria Jessica had initially felt at landing a new job quickly dissipated, and a sense of misery washed over her. She was now officially a stripper. There was no other way of dressing it up. *It's obviously a career choice that runs in the family, seeing as nan was once in that line of work,* Jessica reminded herself as she shoved a handful of chilli peanuts into her mouth. She instantly regretted it as the heat from the chilli seemed intent on skinning the insides of her cheeks. Spluttering, Jessica ran the short distance to the fridge, grabbed a bottle of milk and took a mouthful. She swished it around until the pain receded and her thoughts soon returned to the problem at hand.

Looks like I'm just going to have to put my big girl pants on and stick with stripping until something better comes along. If Jessica was being totally honest with herself, she didn't hold out much hope. Because those were the exact same words she had used when she'd first started working at The Fry Up. And four years later, Jessica had still been there.

Chapter Five

Adriana was relieved she had managed to get to Beatrice's storage room before the cleaners had started in there. It was unbelievable to think that neither her mum or Blossom wanted to go through their mother's personal possessions before they were carted off in rubbish bags to be dumped. The sound from the vacuum cleaner had been non-stop since she'd arrived. What they were hoovering she didn't know, because it wasn't like the apartment was dirty. When Beatrice was alive, she was meticulously clean and had a cleaner come in three times a week. *When she was alive.* Adriana's eyes welled with tears, and she briskly brushed them away with the back of her hand. She was here for a purpose—to fulfil Beatrice's last wish, and she wasn't going to achieve it if she kept getting sentimental at the drop of a hat. With practised ease, Adriana pushed all her thoughts to a back shelf and let herself focus on the task at hand. Adriana had no idea where Beatrice's diaries might be now or whether they were even still in the apartment.

In the corner of the room was a large glass cabinet filled with shelves of old books and a few of her grandad's medals and mementos, so Adriana decided to start there. She went through each book, one at a time, hoping to find the diaries mixed up between them, but to her dismay they weren't there.

Next, she rummaged through the antique desk's drawers and cupboard. Nothing.

When Adriana opened an old chest, and saw it was filled to the top with even more books, she was convinced she would find the diaries amongst them this time, but with great disappointment she came up empty-handed again.

It had been over an hour since her search had begun and Adriana was on the verge of giving up. Stood in the middle of the room with her hands on her hips, Adriana carefully examined every nook and cranny to see if she had missed anything. It was by chance she noticed a briefcase beneath a pile of magazines. Sinking to her knees, she swiped the magazines aside and pulled the case towards her.

They have to be in here.

Joy soon turned to horror when she tried to open it and realised the case was locked by a combination. What made things even worse was the fact that she had no idea what the numbers to open it could be. Not to be a pessimist, Adriana tried the year Beatrice was born, 1-9-3-7. She expectantly pulled at the latch, but it remained firmly closed. Then Adriana tried her grandad's date of birth. Nothing. *Perhaps it's mine.* She tried it but the lock still didn't open. *Obviously not!*

Adriana went through a whole range of years as a possible sequence for the combination lock, starting with her mum's and Aunt Blossom's. She even tried her dad's. When Adriana had no luck with those she moved onto wedding anniversaries, but still the case remained stubbornly locked.

'Guess it's not some kind of date then.' Adriana wanted to scream, but instead let out a frustrated breath as she looked around for something to break the lock open with. As far as she could see there wasn't so much as a screwdriver laying around. Adriana could have gone to the kitchen but she really didn't think she was ready for the onslaught of memories that she knew would come flooding back. Burying her face in her hands she tried to think if Beatrice had ever mentioned any particular numbers to her. *Think, think, think!*

'I've got it!' Adriana suddenly shouted. Giddy with excitement, she remembered a private joke she and Beatrice had often shared. As a child, Adriana had religiously asked Beatrice the ideal age for her to get married when she grew up.

'Somewhere between 18 and 80,' Beatrice had always answered, and Adriana could still remember how Beatrice would throw her head back and laugh. Instinctively, Adriana knew that the numbers making up their little joke were the answer. With bated breath, she entered 1-8-8-0 and pulled the lock. This time it opened easily, and Adriana laughed out loud at her grandmother's ingenuity at choosing a combination only Adriana would be able to figure out.

Inside the case were a stack of small leather bound diaries, and several hand-written poems. Picking up one of the diaries, Adriana flicked through the pages but the adrenaline in her hands made it difficult to hold it steady. Upon seeing how many diaries there were, Adriana knew she would have to study each of the diary's contents thoroughly if she was going to find any information relating to Edwina. But she couldn't do it here, not with so many strangers milling around. Adriana dropped the diary back in the case, locked it and left the room holding it tight against her chest as if it contained the crown jewels.

Adriana was soon at home, sipping coffee as she stared down at the pile of diaries in front of her. Slowly, she turned each page, carefully scanning every written word.

The entries were dated weekly rather than daily, and it seemed that Beatrice had only written down appointments to do with her dentist or bank manager rather than social dates with friends. When Adriana couldn't find anything relating to Edwina, she started to think the diary was a dead end. That was until she got to the last diary where she saw a small heading on the first page, *'Meet Edwina for lunch'*.

The entry was dated 31 January 1962, and Adriana realised that she might finally be on to something. Scanning further down the page, Adriana found what she was looking for—an address in Greenwich with Edwina's name scribbled right next to it.

It was a long shot, going to an address some fifty-five years later, but she knew some people resided at the same address all their lives. In no time at all, Adriana was on the road again heading towards Greenwich. She was excited to meet this mystery woman and perhaps find out why the letter was so important.

Sometime later, Adriana pulled up outside a drab block of flats that looked like they hadn't seen a lick of paint since they were built. Exiting the car like a woman on a mission, she was able to walk straight up to what she hoped was Edwina's apartment on the ground floor and knock on the door.

An elderly man wearing a cap opened it and eyed her suspiciously.

'Hi, sorry to bother you. I'm looking for Edwina Wilson?' Adriana asked hopefully, but the old man just shook his head.

'Never 'eard of her!' he said and slammed the door in her face.

How rude! Adriana was not the type of woman to be easily thrown off track. If the grumpy old man wouldn't help her, she would have to find someone who would. So she knocked next door and on every other door in the small block, asking the same question—did anyone know of Edwina Wilson? Each time she was met with a resounding no. By the time Adriana came to the last flat, she had just about lost all faith.

'I really hope you can help me,' Adriana said almost robotically. 'I'm looking for a lady who used to live in this block. Edwina Wilson?'

The tiny elderly woman frowned slightly.

Adriana let out a long sigh. 'I take it you've never heard of her either. Thanks anyway.'

She turned to go.

'Wait,' The woman said. 'I was just wondering if it

was the same person.'

Adriana turned back, excitement growing by the second. 'Go on.'

'A woman I only knew as Eddy used to live on the ground floor, but that was a few years ago now.'

Eddy? That could be short for Edwina! And only a few years ago! 'Do you have any idea where I might be able to find her? It's very important.'

'I have absolutely no idea. I only know that she always enjoyed traveling … although for the life of me, I never could quite figure out where she got the money from to travel so often. As you can see, we aren't exactly rich folk living here.'

Adriana felt a stab of sadness, and it served to remind her of how much she took her own life for granted. 'Does Edwina have any family that you know of?'

'Yes, dear, she had a granddaughter who used to come around here quite often. A blonde-haired girl. I think her name was Jessica. Yes, that's right, Jessica. She was a teenager then, so she should be around about your age now. Lovely looking thing she was. Always smiling. She came with her dad to see Eddy every weekend.'

'Fantastic! That helps more than you will ever know!' Adriana reached into her pocket to give the woman some money, as was her habit of doing so when someone had done something nice to help her. But her pockets were empty and it was then she remembered why. She was cash-strapped.

'Don't be silly, I don't want anything from you,'

the woman said as if she knew of Adriana's intentions. 'But you could do me a favour and throw a brick through that old bastard's window who took over Eddy's flat. He irritates the hell out of me!'

'I think the best way to get back at him is to shower him with love,' Adriana said before saying goodbye.

She now had something tangible to search for, and if Edwina's neighbour was right, and her granddaughter was in her early twenties, she would probably be on Facebook.

In her car, Adriana did a quick search for Jessica Wilson and prayed that she hadn't got married in the last few years and changed her surname. Thankfully it seemed the gods were now on her side, and she soon located the person who she thought fitted the description of Jessica. She was blonde, and very much as lovely as Edwina's neighbour had pointed out.

It was an added bonus that Jessica made her posts public, so Adriana could see that she worked as a waitress at a cafe called The Fry Up. A quick Google search told her the cafe was in Hackney.

Not one to waste time, Adriana was soon heading across town to Hackney to find the granddaughter of the mysterious woman she was looking for.

Chapter Six

Though the sun shone brightly outside, the curtains were drawn in Jessica's living room, where she sat on her two-seater sofa with a packet of popcorn in hand, absent-mindedly crunching them between her teeth. On the small TV, Colombo was doing his usual routine of outwitting the murderer who thought they could outfox him. The door knocker banged three times, and at first, Jessica ignored it. But when it kept banging, she got to her feet shouting, 'All right, keep your hair on.'

She opened the door and was surprised to see her neighbour standing there with her baby's mouth attached to her exposed nipple.

'Did you hear that those jammy bastards have sold our flats?' Mel asked. A cigarette carelessly hung out the side of her lips.

'No I didn't,' Jessica replied, wishing Mel wouldn't smoke near the baby. No matter how many times she pointed out the dangers, Mel just waved her concern away with a rant about her own mother that smoked around her and how she hadn't come to any harm.

'Well, they have. I hear they're planning on building some bloody shops. So it looks like we're all gonna be out on our arses.'

Jessica didn't really care. She'd been planning on moving out of the dump once she had enough money anyway. The place wasn't fit enough for rats, let alone humans. 'Thanks for letting me know, Mel.'

'No worries. I'm moving in with my mum, so at least I won't be on the street.' Mel gave Jessica a curt nod and walked back to her own flat next door.

Hearing this was all it took to motivate Jessica into looking for new digs. Because if what Mel had said was true, and the flats were being sold underneath their feet, she didn't know how much notice their unscrupulous landlord would give them. Slumping onto her sofa, Jessica picked up her laptop from the floor and typed Rightmove.co.uk into the search bar. Scrolling down past the usual dossholes that wanted extortionate amounts of money for a place you couldn't swing a cat around in, something caught her eye. A spacious one-bedroom apartment for £500 per month, the only negative being it was in need of some tender loving care.

Jessica moved the cursor to the picture and clicked on it. The fact that it was something she would be able to afford astonished her. And as for bringing the place up to scratch, this would be a blessing as Jessica couldn't think of anything she'd like more than to decorate her new pad exactly as she wanted it.

Not wanting to pass up such a golden opportunity, Jessica called the estate agent only to be told that someone would call her back to arrange a viewing. She was disappointed, but it was out of her hands. All she could do was wait. And wait she did. By early evening the estate agent still hadn't called back, so with the little money that she had left, Jessica bought a pizza from the Italian restaurant across the street and took it back home with her to consume. Her mouth watered as the spicy aroma from the pizza drifted up her nostrils.

'You'll never know what I had to go through to find this place! It's like a maze,' a well-spoken female voice sounded from behind Jessica as she fumbled with her key in the lock.

Jessica turned slowly, drawing in a breath as she came face to face with a woman with sleek, jet black hair and dazzling blue eyes that shone like two stars. Her gaze seemed to penetrate deep inside of Jessica, right into the depths of her soul. Strangely, though she felt naked and exposed, Jessica didn't feel violated. The force of the attraction was so overwhelming her hands trembled.

And when the stranger suddenly shot her a dazzling white smile, it was like a burst of sunshine filtering through dark clouds.

'And you are?' Jessica asked when she finally found her voice.

'I'm sorry. I'm being rude. Your manager was kind enough to give me your address when I explained I needed to speak with you about your grandmother Edwina Wilson. My name is Adriana Darrington by the way.'

'I hope you're not a debt collector,' Jessica said with humour. To her relief, the woman's smile didn't falter.

The scent of Chanel No. 5 soon replaced the pizza's aroma as Adriana held out her hand, and Jessica took hold of it. The goose bumps from the contact made the fine hairs on Jessica's arm stand to attention.

'Sorry, I know you told me your name,' Jessica said. 'But you didn't actually say what you wanted.'

'So Edwina is your grandmother, yes.' It was more of a statement than a question.

'She was the last time I checked.'

Adriana let out a long sigh. 'Oh, thank God.'

'Really?' Jessica frowned. 'What's this about?'

'I'm sorry, let me explain—'

'I don't know why, but something tells me this is going to be long-winded. You're welcome to come inside and fill me in while I eat, but I warn you.' Jessica inserted the key in the door and pushed it open. 'My place isn't very big or fancy.'

'I'm just glad I found you,' Adriana said as she followed Jessica inside.

Jessica offered Adriana a slice of pizza, which she declined. As Jessica sat down and bit into a slice, she eyed Adriana who was standing by the doorway giving the room the once over. As hard as she tried, Jessica was unable to stop a stab of lust tearing through her veins.

'Do you actually live in this one room?'

'Yep, cool eh?' Jessica suppressed a laugh at Adriana's bewildered expression. It was obvious she hadn't been in a studio flat before.

'Yes, it's um cosy,' Adriana said politely.

'Okay, out with it then. What do you want to see my nan about?' Jessica dropped her half-eaten pizza back in it's box and leant forward. 'You're a solicitor, aren't you? Oh my God, has my nan inherited some money from a dead relative?'

'No and no,' Adriana said matter-of-factly. 'I have a letter—'

Disappointed, Jessica picked her pizza up again and took a generous bite. 'A letter?'

'Yes, and it needs to be hand delivered to your grandmother. I take it she's still alive?'

'I hope so. But I don't know where she'll be from one minute to the next.' Jessica literally couldn't tear her eyes away from Adriana's hand as she slowly combed her fingers through her hair. It was such a seductive movement that Jessica had to wiggle in her seat to tame the tingling sensations between her thighs.

'I'm not following you,' Adriana said, totally oblivious to the effect she was having on Jessica.

'My nan has a case of wanderlust,' Jessica said trying not to sound as horny as she felt. 'She travels the world all by herself—'

Adriana looked alarmed. 'Surely at her age—'

'What? She should be in bed by eight, drinking cocoa?' Jessica tutted. 'You sound as bad as my dad. Anyway, what I do know is she's not in the country anymore.'

'This is not good. This is not good at all.' Adriana looked unsteady on her feet as she reached for the wall behind her for support.

Jessica was by her side in seconds, taking hold of her elbow and guiding her towards the sofa. 'Sit down. I'll get you something to drink.'

Adriana still looked dazed when Jessica handed her a glass of water.

'What's so important in this letter that it's made you react like this?' Jessica asked, after Adriana had taken a few sips.

Adriana tilted her head to look up at Jessica, and the second their eyes met, Jessica felt as if she had just fallen in love. She shook her head, trying to get rid of such a silly notion. *Love! Don't be so stupid! Lust? Definitely.*

'I can't claim my inheritance until your grandmother has the letter.' Tears welled in Adriana's eyes.

'Shit. That's too bad.' Jessica felt genuinely sorry for her. Adriana seemed like a nice enough person. And she didn't blame her for being upset. If the boot were on the other foot, she'd pretty much feel the same. In fact, she'd be howling.

'Do you have the slightest idea where she is?' Adriana asked before taking another sip of water.

'Unfortunately, my nan doesn't do email and she doesn't have a mobile phone. The last postcard I got was from Australia.'

'Australia's a big country? Which part? Did she mention the hotel she's staying in?' Adriana said. 'Please think.'

'I am.' Jessica pulled a face. 'This is my thinking expression … seriously though, as much as I'd love to help you, I can't. She might have mentioned the hotel but I tossed the card in the bin ages ago.'

'Does your grandmother still have a place here?' Adriana suddenly brightened.

'Yeah, in Islington.'

'Have you got a key?'

Jessica studied Adriana for a moment, wondering what she had in mind. The way Adriana stared back at her unnerved her. Her eyes had the sort of impact only a lover should have. 'My dad has, why?'

'Maybe she left a clue somewhere—'

'You want me to go snooping around my nan's flat? Invading her privacy?' Jessica snorted. 'I don't think so—'

'Not even for fifty grand?'

Jessica quickly broke eye contact, before she got drawn in any further. 'Yeah, right, like you've got fifty grand to be splashing around.'

Adriana put her glass on the table, got to her feet, and walked over to the window. 'Come and take a look.'

Jessica joined her, glad for the opportunity to be close to her again, but at the same time grateful she didn't have to face her. 'What am I looking at?'

'See that red car down there?'

Jessica slowly looked from left to right until she spotted the red car. Her eyes automatically widened. 'The Ferrari?'

'It's mine, in case you're thinking I don't have the means to make good on the fifty grand.'

Don't look at her, don't look at her, but Jessica's mind wouldn't obey. It was an overwhelming compulsion. She just had to look. Jessica turned to her and Adriana's eyes stared back intensely. Jessica's stomach fluttered and she quickly switched her gaze back to the car. 'That could be anyone's for all I know.'

'Only one way to find out.' Adriana took out her

car keys and dangled them in front of Jessica. 'Let's go for a spin!'

It wasn't until Jessica was actually sat on the luxury leather seat that she believed Adriana was telling the truth and she actually owned the Ferrari. Buckling herself in, Jessica felt like she had been caught up in a dream and any minute now she would wake up and Colombo would just be coming to an end.

'Ready?' Adriana asked, giving her a sideways glance.

Jessica smiled and nodded her head as Adriana inserted the key and started the engine. Adriana floored the accelerator and the car went forward like a rocket being launched. Adrenaline shot through Jessica's body.

'I can't believe this is actually all real!' Jessica shouted above the engines roar.

Adriana laughed.

As they sped across London, Jessica tried to imagine how it would feel to live like this. Driving around in a car that she wouldn't be able to afford in two lifetimes. Being with a woman that could probably make steel melt if she looked at it long enough.

Just thinking about her eyes alone made Jessica shiver in delight.

Adriana stopped the car at the traffic lights. 'Do you believe me now?'

'That you own this car? Yep, I can tell it's yours by the way you handle it.'

'I hope that's a compliment.'

'It is,' Jessica said, wondering if Adriana was as

confident in bed as she was behind the wheel. She paused her thoughts to give herself a mental slap for even going down that road. Adriana probably had a billionaire boyfriend, not fiancé, because she'd already checked out her wedding finger. And even if she wasn't attached, what was the likelihood of Adriana wanting to see her again. It wasn't as if they moved in the same circles and could become friends. So far her gaydar hadn't gone off. But that wasn't surprising. Jessica was useless when it came to sussing out other lesbians.

Even so, Jessica didn't want to part company just yet. All that awaited her at home was a cold pizza and the TV. Neither were as exciting as this. With this in mind, Jessica weighed up the pros and cons of taking Adriana to her nan's place. If she took her there it would mean she would get to spend more time with Adriana. *That in itself is more than enough*. And the cons? She couldn't think of a single one.

'Turn right at the next lights.' Jessica suddenly heard herself say. It seemed her mind had made its decision without her input. 'It's the way to my nan's place.'

Adriana looked at her and Jessica wished she wouldn't. Her eyes did things to Jessica that she didn't think were possible.

'I thought your dad had the key.'

'He does.' Jessica looked out of the window. 'But I know where the spare one is.'

'Great, let's do this,' Adriana said, expertly taking the corner.

Jessica didn't think she'd ever arrived at a destination so quickly in her life. One minute they were in Hackney and then in what felt like nanoseconds, Adriana was bringing the car to a stop outside her nan's flat in Islington.

'It's nice to get a taste of how the other half live.' Jessica reluctantly climbed out of the car. If she could, she would have remained in it all night, especially with Adriana by her side.

Jessica gestured for Adriana to wait on the path while she walked across the garden and picked up a garden ornament disguised as a rock. Removing the key from inside, Jessica held it up in the air and smiled when she saw the relief on Adriana's face.

Once they were inside the apartment, Jessica set about looking through Edwina's mail. 'I feel like I'm snooping.'

'Just think of how happy your grandmother will be when she gets the letter,' Adriana said, looking through a pile of magazines on the glass coffee table.

'How do we even know it's going to make her happy? Your nan might be slagging my nan off for something she did decades ago.'

'My grandmother—'

'Would never do that. I know. I actually think bitching's a modern thing. Back in our nan's day they actually had a life.'

'Look,' Adriana said suddenly.

Jessica turned to look at her and saw that she was holding a travel brochure—*Destination Australia*. 'Let me have a look.'

Adriana handed it to her and Jessica flicked through it, stopping when she got to the page where her nan had scribbled a few notes next to the Soft Rainbow guesthouse. 'Hey, I remember now. This is where she said she was staying.'

'Where?' Adriana said coming to her side.

'At this guesthouse in Sydney.' Jessica didn't know how it could have slipped her mind considering what was at stake.

Adriana pinched the bridge of her nose. 'And there I was thinking delivering her letter was going to be easy.'

'Nothing in life is easy,' Jessica said, mentally saying goodbye to her fifty grand.

'I am so buggered,' Adriana said with resignation.

'Maybe not.' Jessica took her phone out of her pocket. 'I'll call the hotel and see if I can get through to her. Then I can find out when she's coming back.'

'That will be a great help,' Adriana said as Jessica called the guesthouse.

A few minutes later they were back to square one. 'They said they can't give out personal information.'

Adriana let out a frustrated sigh, but said nothing.

'If you give me your number I'll call you the minute I hear from her,' Jessica said, feeling an overpowering need to keep Adriana in her life.

'I suppose,' Adriana said in a lacklustre tone.

'Look, I know I don't know you or anything, but do you want to come back to mine for a drink?' Jessica tossed the brochure on the table. 'I hate to think of you being alone when you're upset.'

Adriana gave her a penetrating look and Jessica's legs trembled beneath her.

'Who said I'd be alone?' Adriana said.

'Oh sorry, I meant, I ….'

Adriana was already heading for the door. 'Come on, I'll drop you home … And thanks for trying.'

'I wish I could have done more.'

The drive back to Jessica's flat was sombre. Even the car seemed sluggish as it moved along the road. When they arrived at Jessica's flat, she unclipped her seat belt, but made no attempt to get out. 'If you ever need anything, you know where I live. For the next few weeks anyway.'

'Are you moving?' Adriana asked politely.

Jessica nodded.

'That's good to hear. I'd be frightened to death having to come home in the dark.'

Jessica shrugged. 'You know what they say, beggars can't be choosers.'

'I suppose not.' Adriana's gaze fell on the door then back to Jessica. 'Well thanks again. And good luck with your move.'

Jessica took the hint that Adriana wanted her to make a quick exit. 'Yeah, you too.'

For some inexplicable reason, Jessica felt as if her heart had been squeezed so hard it hurt. She had barely been in Adriana's company for an hour but the impact she'd made on her was enormous. Letting herself into her gloomy room, Jessica glanced over at the pizza box.

It seemed like a lifetime ago that Adriana was in her living room.

Reality strikes again. TV for the next hour then bed! Sometimes she didn't even know why she bothered getting up in the morning. Jessica flipped open the pizza box, grateful she didn't mind eating it cold and took a big bite of a slice. Just then a rapid tap sounded at the front door. Thinking it was Mel from next door, she took her time answering it.

'Now what is—'

Pulling open the door and seeing Adriana standing there caused her to take a quick intake of breath. As she did so, the pizza she had taken a bite of shot towards the back of her mouth and before she could stop it, lodged in her throat. Jessica began choking. In a panic, she stepped back, practically throwing herself against the wall in an attempt to dislodge the dough. Before Jessica realised what was happening, Adriana's hands were on her shoulders spinning her round. Then she felt Adriana's arms wrap themselves around her stomach, squeezing her so tight the piece of pizza automatically popped out of Jessica's mouth.

'Fuck, I thought I was a goner then.' Jessica gave Adriana a cocksure grin when she'd recovered from the shock of what had just happened. 'You saved my life.'

Adriana eyeballed her as if she couldn't tell if she was being serious or not. 'If I hadn't surprised you, you wouldn't have choked on your food. Cause and effect.'

'Yeah, that's true.' Jessica briefly looked down at her remaining pizza in disgust. 'Do you need to use the toilet or something?'

'The toilet?' Adriana looked perplexed.

'Yeah, I mean you were on your way home—'

'Are you asking me indirectly why I came back up? You could just ask outright you know.'

Jessica's cheeks reddened. 'Sorry, I didn't want to appear rude.'

Adriana waved away her apology. 'If you think being honest is rude you'd never have survived growing up in my house.'

'Mmm sounds like fun.' Jessica couldn't even begin to imagine what it would be like growing up in a home where everyone spoke their minds. Yes, she could, *it would be horrific, that's what it would be.*

'You get used to it,' Adriana said as if she'd just read Jessica's mind.

'In that case, what do you want?' Jessica inwardly cringed. Being straightforward didn't sit comfortably with her at all. She actually liked the British way of lying through their teeth rather than offending someone. Unless it was Ben, her tight-fisted boss that is.

'See doesn't that feel better?' Adriana said.

'Honestly?' Jessica grimaced. 'No it doesn't.'

'You'll get used to it. Anyway,' Adriana clasped her hands together, 'I have a proposal for you.'

'I'm all ears.'

'Are you sure you've got nothing in your mouth to choke on?'

Jessica stuck her tongue out and moved it anti-clockwise. 'I'm sure.'

'Good, because I'm going to Sydney to find your grandmother.' She paused. 'And seeing as she won't know me from Adam, I want you to come with me.'

Jessica was speechless. All she could do was burst out laughing. *She's obviously lost her grip on reality.* There could be no other explanation. 'Pull the other one.'

Adriana folded her arms across her chest. 'I'm not with you—'

'Listen, Adriana, and this time I will be perfectly frank with you. I'm sure in your circle of friends popping on a plane to Oz might seem like just another little jaunt, but in my reality, Oz is the sort of place you spend years saving up to visit. And I mean years!' she repeated with emphasis.

'If you would have let me finish, I was going to say flights and expenses will be paid for by me. And ….'

Jessica opened her mouth to speak and Adriana held up her hand to silence her.

'And I will raise the fee to a hundred thousand pounds.'

Jessica gulped. 'A hundred grand? Are you having me on?'

'Why would I do that?'

A hundred grand? Sydney? Jessica's bearings were so bad she wouldn't be able to pinpoint Australia on a map if her life depended on it. Even her geography teacher at school had lost patience with her and gave up trying to instil in her a sense of the world outside the UK.

'So let me get this straight. You're going to give me a hundred grand—'

'When we find your grandmother,' Adriana cut in.

'And not only pay for my flight to Sydney but my accommodation as well?' Jessica continued as if Adriana hadn't spoken. 'I'd be a mug to say no but ... I'm meant to be starting a new job next week.'

'We should be back by then. We know where your grandmother is staying,' Adriana said with conviction. 'We find her. I deliver the letter then we come back. Just in time for you to start your new job.'

In her mind's eye Jessica saw herself on stage under Micky's leery gaze. If she had a hundred grand, the Sleazy Slum was the last place on earth she would return to. 'Well ....'

'Is there something else holding you back? Like a partner or something?'

'No nothing like that,' Jessica said, taking a moment to think about Adriana's plan. Even if Jessica didn't find her nan, she would still get a free trip to Australia *with Adriana*. And if they did locate her, she'd be in the money and all of her immediate problems would be solved. In other words, it was a win-win for Jessica whatever the outcome.

'Sod it, you've twisted my arm. I'll come.'

Jessica saw the tension flood out of Adriana's features. 'That's the spirit!'

'So when do we leave?'

'A couple of days? The quicker we find her the ....' Adriana paused and looked thoughtful for a moment. 'What happens if we're in Australia and your grandmother sends another postcard here to your flat? She might have moved to another hotel before we get there.'

Jessica knew the solution to that problem. Ariel was still living with her parents in a two-bedroom flat. She would jump at the chance to house sit Jessica's place even if it was a dosshole.

'Let me make a call,' Jessica said, punching Ariel's number into her phone. 'Hey, Ariel, how would you feel about house sitting for me? Yes, my place. Probably a few days. No it's got nothing to do with me quitting my job. So what do you think? Great! All I need you to do is let me know if any snail mail arrives from my nan.'

Jessica loved the way Ariel was prepared to just jump right in without asking a hundred questions.

'I take it she said yes,' Adriana said, lowering herself onto the sofa when Jessica hung up.

'She sure did.' Jessica stared at Adriana and for a brief moment she was overcome with the desire to walk over to her and kiss her right on her delectable mouth. *I'd probably give the poor woman a heart attack in the process.*

Instead, Jessica said nonchalantly, 'You're welcome to crash here tonight and we can get things rolling in the morning.'

Adriana flashed her a grateful smile. 'Thanks, I really didn't feel like driving all the way back to Chelsea tonight.'

'Great, so do you fancy a drink?' Jessica asked hopefully. She wasn't ready to end the evening so soon.

'I should get some sleep. It's going to be a busy day tomorrow.'

Jessica was disappointed but at the same time she

realised Adriana was right. Besides, there'd be plenty of time for drinks and late nights after tomorrow.

'You can sleep on the bed. I'll kip on the sofa.'

'Absolutely not. I'll be fine here.'

Jessica pulled Adriana up by the hand. 'I insist.'

It was easier parting with her knowing she was only going to be a few feet away. Why Jessica felt this way about Adriana she didn't know. But she was sure it would only be a matter of time before she found out.

Chapter Seven

Adriana wasn't surprised Jessica's pull-down bed was very uncomfortable. It was lumpy and springs poked her ribcage wherever her position. Doubling up the quilt, she lay on top of it and thought about her own comfortable super king-size bed that was empty and waiting for her. Adriana would have gone home but she had decided to stay on instinct. Adriana didn't know Jessica and was worried if she let her out of her sight, Jessica might change her mind about going to Sydney with her. Not that Adriana would blame her. Who in their right mind would travel half way across the world with someone they didn't know, just to hand deliver a letter? *Someone who's desperate.*

In fact, everything about Jessica's 'flat' screamed desperation, from the threadbare carpet to the peeling paint, not to mention the claustrophobic living room/bedroom. Adriana could barely breathe and she had only been there an hour. The thought of actually living there was unimaginable. It was disturbing that Adriana's own bathroom was nearly the size of Jessica's whole flat.

Thinking of Jessica laying a few feet away on the sofa, Adriana couldn't help but smile. She'd liked her instantly. Besides the obvious fact that Jessica was very attractive, Adriana liked that she was confident without being cocky. Amusing without being overbearing. And she radiated a real warmth that seemed to be genuine. A far cry from the women Adriana normally surrounded herself with.

In reality, Adriana could have just as easily gone to Australia by herself, but for some reason she found herself wanting to spend time with Jessica. A normal woman who was not bound and hypothetically gagged by a societal straight jacket.

Curling into a ball, Adriana focused on the sound of the rain lashing against the window. She found herself hypnotised by the urgency of the downfall and without even realising, her thoughts slowly faded into silence.

Abba blared from next door and Adriana was yanked out of her dream. She'd been dreaming that Edwina and Beatrice were in a brightly lit room and Beatrice, in a flowing white gown, was asking Edwina to join her. To go somewhere with her. Beatrice was smiling and Edwina smiled back. In that moment, Adriana could feel a bond between the two women that was stronger than life itself. That whatever had bound them together in life would follow them into the afterlife. Her eyes glowing, Beatrice mouthed something to Edwina but Adriana couldn't make out what she'd said.

Groaning, Adriana lay on her front and pulled the pillow over her head to muffle the noise, but it was pointless. The moment had fully passed and she was firmly back in the present. Now she would never know what Beatrice had been trying to tell her. Was Edwina no longer on the earthly plane?

Giving up on the idea of trying to go back to sleep and recapturing the dream, Adriana rolled out of bed and headed for the bathroom door. Pulling it back, she was surprised to see Jessica. Adriana's eyes involuntarily roamed over Jessica's body, who was wearing black boxers and a matching bra. An unexpected flush of desire left Adriana stunned. She felt faint with longing.

Well aware that her eyes would reveal all, Adriana swallowed hard, fixing her gaze on the ground.

'I take it from the look on your face you're either not an Abba fan or an early riser?' Jessica said.

Adriana was relieved Jessica hadn't guessed the real reason for avoiding her gaze. 'Let's just say I'd appreciate Abba more if it was midnight and I was in a nightclub … drunk.'

Jessica grinned. 'Yeah I know what you mean. Now you're up, do you want a coffee?'

'Sure.' Adriana gradually looked up, feeling more composed now. 'Thank you.'

'Nescafe all right?' Jessica brushed past her causing Adriana's entire body to tingle.

Adriana nodded, choosing to ignore the feeling Jessica's touch had elicited. For all she knew, Jessica could have a boyfriend and would be totally freaked out if another woman unexpectedly came on to her.

'I'd better get some clothes on first,' Jessica said as if suddenly aware she was standing around in her underwear.

'Do you mind if I take a shower?'

'Treat the place like your own. Clean towels are on

the radiator.'

After a lukewarm shower, Adriana made her way back to the living room. As she passed the slightly ajar front door, she could see Jessica talking to another woman with thick, dark curly hair. By the time Jessica brought the woman in to meet her, Adriana was fully dressed and in the process of applying her lipstick.

'Adriana this is my friend Ariel,' Jessica said, gesturing to the pretty woman.

'Nice to meet you,' Adriana said, dropping her lipstick in her bag.

'You too,' Ariel replied, with a bemused expression on her face as she looked from Adriana to Jessica.

'Here's your coffee,' Jessica said.

'Thanks.' Adriana didn't miss the baleful look Jessica shot at Ariel before Jessica handed Adriana her drink.

'I'm so excited to have some space for myself!' Ariel beamed as she looked around the cramped room. Whatever message Jessica had tried to get across to her seemed to have worked. Ariel's attention was no longer on the women but her new home.

'Right. I'd better head off and make arrangements for the flights. I take it you have a passport?' Adriana asked Jessica. She made a silent prayer that her answer would be yes. If it wasn't, Adriana didn't know what she would do. Go by herself? If that's what it came down to, she'd have to.

'Right here.' Jessica took her passport from her

back pocket and handed it to her.

Adriana flipped it open at the back. She couldn't help but smile seeing Jessica's picture. She stared into the camera with an almost petrified expression on her face.

'Yes, I know it's awful,' Jessica said.

Adriana closed the passport. 'Mine isn't much better.'

'That I find hard to believe,' Jessica said.

Now this is what confused Adriana. The indirect flirting. Which made her think Jessica might be gay. After all, straight women didn't normally compliment each other in that way. Not the women she knew anyway. Neither did other women blush the way Jessica did whenever Adriana looked at her. *Unless she's just shy.* 'Do you mind if I take the passport number down to book the flights?'

Jessica quickly scribbled the number on a scrap of paper as well as her date of birth and address. 'There're all of my details.'

'Great, so I'll call you later once I've made all the arrangements,' Adriana said.

'Yep, speak to you later then,' Jessica said.

Adriana remained rooted to the spot. She didn't want to leave. Not yet. Not without Jessica. In her heart, she wished they were leaving for Sydney that day, but she had to talk to her parents about paying for the tickets. Another twenty-four hours seemed so far away. Realising how she felt, shocked Adriana to the core. She had never had attachment issues in her life. Even her own mother had said that Adriana was an independent baby, never wanting to be fussed over and preferring to be left to her own devices. So why was she now feeling sad at the thought of leaving Jessica?

'Is something wrong?' Jessica asked when Adriana didn't leave.

'No, just finishing my coffee,' she lied. It was the foulest thing she had ever tasted.

'Oh right. Suppose I'd better nip down to the chemist and get my supplies,' Jessica said. 'Be back in a while, Ariel.'

Adriana left with Jessica. There wasn't any reason to hang around if she wasn't going to be there. They said their goodbyes at the bottom of the stairwell then both went their separate ways. By the time Adriana went home to change and drove over to her parents' house, it was nearly 11 a.m.

'How are you, Mum?' Adriana said, giving Alice a brief hug.

'Slowly adjusting to the new reality without your grandmother,' Alice replied, her voice breaking slightly.

Drawing back, Adriana noticed the dark shadows under her eyes and the new worry lines on her forehead. Alice seemed to have aged slightly, all in the space of a few weeks. Stress caused such drastic reactions in the body, and it never failed to amaze Adriana. A friend at university had to drop out of her course because she found the work too hard to deal with. Her symptoms first started with weight loss and tiredness only to then explode into a red rash which covered her from head to toe. The doctors couldn't find a cause for it and it was only when she returned to the comfort of the family home did it mysteriously disappear.

So maybe a few lines here and there didn't amount to much but Adriana was more concerned with what the stress was doing internally to her mother.

'I know what you mean. But we've got to be thankful she didn't suffer. She had a full, rich life, right up until the end.' Adriana gently squeezed Alice's shoulders.

When Adriana returned from Sydney she would spend some quality time with her mother. If it was one thing she had learnt from Beatrice's sudden death, it was that each second was precious and so were your loved ones.

'I know you're right,' Alice said with a sad smile. 'I should be grateful. Some people aren't lucky enough to have their mother around until eighty.'

'I hope I'm going to be one of the lucky ones,' Adriana said, not wanting to even think about Alice not being there one day.

'So how's your search going?' Alice asked, briskly changing the subject. 'Any idea where this mystery woman is yet?'

'Not really, but the good news is I found her granddaughter.' An image of Jessica's near naked body popped up in her mind's eye and warmth spread throughout her.

'And the bad news?'

'Her grandmother's in Australia.' Adriana could

tell by Alice's fretful expression that she believed Adriana's search for Edwina had been in vain.

'Does she live there?'

Adriana shook her head. 'It seems Edwina Wilson likes to travel.'

'When is she back?'

Adriana took a seat at the table and picked up a biscuit from the plate. She bit into it and chewed slowly. 'That's just it. Jessica doesn't know.'

Alice raised her eyebrows. 'Jessica?'

'Edwina's granddaughter.'

'Is she married?'

Alice joined her at the table and Adriana knew they were going to have one of their talks. The one in which Alice regurgitated her disappointment that Adriana couldn't have been more like her other friends who were now married and settled in their lives.

'I can't help but feel sad that you're still single,' Alice said.

Her words were like salt water poured onto an open wound. 'And not happily married with two children, a house in Kensington and one in the South of France—'

'Which is exactly what you'll have when you marry Hugo Legaurd. I think he's been very patient with you. Why won't you just say yes to him?'

The lie that left Adriana's mouth was more to protect Alice than anything else. The last thing she wanted to do was put any more stress on her already weary shoulders. And that's exactly what she would do if she told her the truth about how she really felt. 'Mum, I can't think about anything but delivering Granny's letter at the moment.'

'You can't put it off forever, darling. You have to make sacrifices for the greater good.'

Adriana felt deflated. 'And marrying Hugo is for the greater good?'

'Yes, being married will help you. I know you'll get your inheritance but the way you spend money it will be gone in no time. Hugo will give you the stability and security you need.' Alice gave her a tense smile. 'That's what every woman needs—'

'You're starting to sound like we've been transported back to the fifties.'

'Okay, I'll drop it but only if you promise me you'll agree to marry him soon,' Alice said. 'Your father is just as impatient as I am for—'

'Speaking of Dad, where is he?'

'At the art gallery. He wants to buy some godawful paintings from a new artist.' Alice's face crumpled as if she'd just sucked on a lemon. 'So back to Edwina. What are you going to do? Wait until she returns to England?'

'No I can't. I need to find her—'

'Look, if it's about the money—'

'It's not about the money, Mum. I want to do this for Granny.' She reached into her pocket and took out the piece of paper with Jessica's details. 'Can you ask Dad to book me two tickets to Australia for tomorrow please. I'll pay it back ASAP.'

Both Adriana and Alice looked up startled at the

male voice booming from the hallway. When Hugo appeared in the doorway, a wide smile spread across Alice's face and she jumped up to greet him, wrapping her arms halfway around his broad shoulders.

If Adriana didn't know better she would have thought Alice was secretly in love, or at the very least infatuated, with Hugo herself. Not that she could blame her. Hugo was impossibly handsome with a great physique, thick dark hair and green eyes that no doubt made women weak at the knees. He was the type of man that women dreamt of.

Just not me.

And no matter how many times she wished it could be, Adriana just never felt that spark in her heart. In all the time she had known Hugo, Adriana had never once fantasised about what it would be like to have him touch her, or to lay naked with him, skin to skin. To be excited at the mere thought of being intimate with him. But she had already had these thoughts about Jessica. A woman she had barely known for twenty-four hours.

Hugo released Alice from their embrace and looked expectantly at Adriana. Dutifully, she rose to her feet, and on tiptoes pecked his cheek. Before she could step back, Hugo slid his arm around her waist and pulled her tight against his rock-hard chest.

'What are you doing here?' Adriana pulled away as naturally as she could without seeming awkward.

His eyes never left hers. 'I saw your car outside, so I thought I'd pop in for a chat.'

Adriana inwardly groaned. She knew what this

'chat' would entail. He was just as bad as Alice, in that he thought it was time for them to become engaged. The only difference being, he wasn't as obvious. Hugo tended to skirt around the issue. Dropping hints about wanting to settle down and find himself a good wife, or a family house he had seen in the estate agent's window. A mutual friend's wedding he had attended. How quickly time was passing by and they were getting older. And each time, Adriana had nodded politely and agreed with him when necessary, all the while praying that he would meet the woman of his dreams and give her a break.

Adriana grabbed her keys from the table. 'I'd love to but I was just leaving. Some other time?'

'But—'

'I'm sure my mum would love for you to stay. She was just about to put the kettle on. Weren't you, Mum?' Adriana backed away towards the door.

Alice looked perplexed before it finally dawned on her that Adriana was asking her for back up.

'Hugo, I was just about to prepare some lunch,' Alice said with a gleam in her eyes. 'I'm making your favourite. Scallops.'

Adriana could see Hugo was trying to mask his disappointment with a smile but she really didn't have the time or the desire to sit around talking about a future she had no wish to be a part of.

'In that case, I'll stay. Nothing to stop us discussing a few things between us, is there, Alice?'

Adriana heard the intent in his voice. *That's right,*

make decisions about my life as if what I want doesn't matter.

'I'll catch up with you some other time,' Adriana said, then left them to it.

Chapter Eight

Checking the inside of her suitcase one more time, Jessica rummaged through her clothes and toiletries to make sure she hadn't forgotten anything. She could tell Adriana was getting impatient by the way she planted her hands on her hips and let out frustrated sighs now and again, but Jessica wasn't going to be rushed.

'You do know we're going to a city, Jessica. They have shops where you can buy things. It won't be the end of the world if you forget something.'

'Sorry. I'm done now.' Jessica started to zip her case shut. When she stalled momentarily, Adriana shot her a warning glance that told her not to even think of opening the case again.

Getting to her feet, Jessica pulled the case up by the handle. She turned around to take one final look at the place. It was going to be strange not waking up in the depressing room. And though it should have made her happy, it didn't. The thought of being thousands of miles away from her comfort zone scared the living daylights out of her. It was all right for Adriana. She lived the jet set lifestyle, travelling from country to country with her rich friends. Adriana didn't know what it was like to have gone through the same routine for years.

As if sensing Jessica's apprehension, Adriana took hold of the handle and dragged it outside.

With one last look at the place she called home,

Jessica followed, locking the door behind her. Ariel was at work and wouldn't be back until midnight, so she couldn't give Jessica one more pep talk on how everything was going to be all right.

The previous night, until the early hours of the morning, Ariel had reassured her that the plane's engines wouldn't drop off. That there wouldn't be an on-board fire. Yes, there would be several pilots and not just one to make the twenty-two-hour journey. Whatever fear she had thrown at Ariel, Ariel had countered with answers that made Jessica less anxious.

However, the only thing she couldn't advise her on was Adriana. Despite Jessica not knowing whether Adriana batted for the same side or not, there was no denying that Adriana felt something for her. Jessica would have had to be pretty clueless not to have picked up on the way Adriana had eyed her in the hallway the day before. Not being one to boast, but Jessica knew when someone was attracted to her, and unless she had completely got it wrong, the signs were there that Adriana was into her. Whether she would admit it, that was another matter altogether. In the end, Ariel had suggested to just play it by ear, which is what Jessica intended to do.

'I have to keep pinching myself to make sure I'm not dreaming!' Jessica said, more out of fear than excitement. The nearer they got to the airport the more dread she felt. What if something happened to her mum or dad while she was away? What if her nan had left Oz and the journey turned out to be a complete and utter waste of time? What if the plane crashed?

What if? What if? What if?

'Have you been on a plane before?' Adriana suddenly asked, making Jessica think her fear was now visible despite her trying to contain it by keeping her hands clenched in her lap.

'The furthest I've been out of London is to Brighton. The only reason I even have a passport is for ID purposes.'

'Then you're in for a pleasant surprise. I know you must be nervous but just try and relax. I won't let anything happen to you,' Adriana said, giving Jessica's knee a reassuring squeeze.

Jessica's heart elevated at her touch. *Apart from give me a heart attack that is.*

The sign post to the airport gave them directions to take the next exit, which Adriana did. She then continued until they saw the sign to the 'meet and greet' car parking area in terminal one.

Jessica felt a spasm of alarm just seeing the word terminal. Couldn't the airport planners have thought up a word less scary, less telling? Hinting at the fact this could be the beginning of the end for passengers was a bit of a piss take as far as she was concerned.

For a split second, Jessica thought Adriana's own nerves were showing, that was until she realised she wasn't scared of the flight, more likely the intention the car attendant had for her car. The way his eyes slowly roamed over the car's sleek red body even had Jessica wondering what perversions were going through his mind. She had seen a documentary about people having sex 'with' cars, so her way of thinking wasn't that far-fetched.

After reluctantly handing over the car keys, they took the lift to the lower floor and made their way over to departures. It was by seeing so many people that Jessica's nervousness began to wane. It felt a bit like safety in numbers. If so many people wanted to take a flight it couldn't be that bad.

With renewed confidence, Jessica walked beside Adriana with a huge grin on her face as she imagined the luxury that awaited them. Adriana didn't strike her as the type of woman who slummed it in economy or cattle class as she'd often heard it referred to. No, it was going to be an experience she was never going to forget. From what she'd seen on TV about flying first class it was going to be champagne and comfort all the way.

'This is one of the benefits of flying first class,' Adriana said as they strode past a massive queue for economy flights.

'Cool.' Jessica felt like a star, especially when the agent greeted them with the kind of respect she'd only seen given to VIPs.

'When we check in we'll go straight to the first-class lounge and have a few drinks and something to eat.'

Adriana held out her hand for Jessica's passport and with her own passed it to the ticket agent who beamed as she looked down and typed in the details. Just as quickly as the smile had appeared, it vanished.

'You're in the wrong queue. This is for first class

passengers only.'

'Pardon?' Adriana said as if the agent had said something dirty to her. 'My father booked two first class tickets to Sydney.'

'Your tickets say economy,' she said.

'There's got to be a mistake.'

'Not on my system there isn't. If you think there's been a misunderstanding, I suggest you get in touch with whoever booked your ticket.'

'I will,' Adriana said, taking the passports back from the agent before retrieving her phone from her pocket and walking away.

Jessica remained standing close enough to hear Adriana's conversation but far away not to intrude.

'Dad, there seems to be a problem with the plane tickets. No they're there but the ticket agent said they were for economy. She's right? What do you mean she's right? Dad, I've never flown in economy in my life. Can you put Mum on? Hello? Hello? Dad?'

Adriana looked down at her phone in disbelief before turning to face Jessica. 'He hung up on me. I can't believe it.'

Neither could Jessica as she watched her dreams of luxury go up in flames. In a way, Jessica felt sorry for Adriana as she ate humble pie when they joined the back of the queue for economy. An hour later, when they walked through to security she noticed how Adriana avoided looking at the passengers who were walking straight through.

'Hey, come on, cheer up. This is my first time in

an airport, I wouldn't have wanted to sit in a lounge anyway.'

Adriana shot her an apologetic smile. 'I'm sorry, you're right. I'm spoiling your experience. What would you like to do?'

'Oh, can we go and have a drink in that fancy restaurant over there? My treat. I cashed out all my savings for this trip,' Jessica said excitedly when they finally got through security.

'Why did you do that?'

'Because I'm not a ponce. I don't have much but I'll pay towards whatever I can. And you,' she looped her arm through Adriana's, 'look like you need a strong drink. If you play your cards right, I'll buy you two.'

'The last of the big spenders,' Adriana said with humour.

Jessica grinned. 'That's me.'

Jessica went to the bar while Adriana found them an empty table. When the barman presented her with a bill for twenty quid for two drinks she nearly fainted. For the next round, she would get tap water for herself.

'So have you been tempted to open the letter to my nan and have a peek?' Jessica asked once she was seated.

'Once. But I'm sure if she wanted the contents to be known she would have left it open.'

'I suppose,' Jessica said, taking a minuscule sip of her drink. She needed it to last as long as possible. 'I forgot to ask what your nan's name was?'

'Beatrice. Do you ever remember meeting someone

by that name when you were visiting your grandmother?'
Adriana asked.

'I don't think so.'

'Perhaps your grandmother called her Bea?'

'Nah, still doesn't ring a bell.'

Adriana took a leisurely sip of her drink and
Jessica looked on in dismay as the level of wine lowered.
If Adriana kept drinking at the speed she was going,
Jessica reasoned she'd be broke before they even got on
the plane.

'How long ago did your grandmother leave for
Sydney?'

'About two weeks ago.'

Adriana drained her glass. 'Your grandmother
must be very wealthy if she can afford to travel the
world.'

'That's just it, she isn't. My nan was financially
strapped, and then one day she told us she was going to
the Bahamas. Just like that. She never said how she was
paying for it. We all assumed she'd won a few thousand
on the lottery or something.'

Adriana stood up. 'Mmm, I wonder if she got the
money from my grandmother?'

'It would explain her sudden change of fortune,'
Jessica said and took another small sip of her wine. 'But
why on earth would she give my nan money?'

'My grandmother never needed a reason to do any
of the things she did.' Adriana picked up her glass.
'Another?'

'I'll get it.'

'It's fine. I'll get a bottle.'

'Are you sure?'

'Absolutely.'

By the time a voice over the tannoy called for passengers for Sydney to start boarding at gate eight, Jessica couldn't care less if the plane crashed. If she was going to die beside this awesome woman she couldn't think of a better way to go. Whether that was the drink talking she didn't know or care. All she knew was that the longer she spent with Adriana the more in awe she was of her. And best of all Jessica could look her directly in the eyes now and she didn't care that her nervous system went into freefall. In fact, she welcomed it wholeheartedly.

'We'd better get going.' Adriana grabbed her bag as she got to her feet.

'I can't wait,' Jessica said draining the last dregs of wine from her glass.

'Really?' Adriana didn't look entirely convinced at Jessica's sudden change of heart.

'Really, come on. Sydney here we come!'

They boarded the plane and Adriana led the way along the aisle to their seats in the last row. After watching the safety presentation, Jessica clipped the belt on, checked she knew where her life jacket was, *just in case*, then stared out of her window and watched the runway gradually disappear beneath them as the plane took off.

Jessica had never felt so excited or exhilarated in her entire life. *Apart from the day I met Adriana that is.*

Chapter Nine

Adriana tried to get comfortable in her seat. It was worse than she could have ever imagined. *And to think people actually pay money to travel like this.* She glanced down the aisle at the heavy blue curtain that separated the cabins. There'd be no private pod on this flight. No gourmet meal. Nor a fully reclining chair, or chilled champagne before take-off.

Adriana wished her father could see her now and what she was being subjected to. Sitting in a chair where she could barely stretch her legs out in front of her. No, not barely, she couldn't full stop. The thought of being scrunched up for hours filled her with dread. But it was something she would have to endure. And she would suffer in silence. The last thing Adriana wanted was to make Jessica's first flight a miserable one. Especially seeing her sitting there like a kid in a candy store. Because Jessica hadn't flown first class before, she was oblivious to the true comfort of such an experience.

The pilot switched the seat belt sign off and before long an air hostess pushing a trolley stopped by them. Jessica asked for a bottle of wine and Adriana two bottles of water. She knew only too well the effects of drinking on a long-haul flight and tried to avoid alcohol once she'd boarded the plane. It was all too easy to drink non-stop without realising the true amount consumed. Without being too obvious Adriana would keep a check on how much Jessica was drinking and make sure she drank a lot of water to prevent her from becoming dehydrated.

'Have you lived in London your entire life?' Adriana asked once the air hostess moved on.

'Yep,' Jessica said. Her eyes were still glassy with excitement even though the flight had been going for more than an hour. 'My mum and dad still live in the same house I was born in.'

'When you say born in, I take it you don't mean it literally,' Adriana said, dreading the thought of Jessica's mother giving birth to her without the assistance of a medical team. Though some women opted for home births she didn't think she would ever be brave enough to be one of them.

'Yeah I do. My dad delivered me. The ambulance didn't arrive in time. Seems the NHS was on its knees even back then.'

'That was very brave of your dad. It's nice your parents are still together.'

'Are yours?'

'Very much so,' Adriana said. 'They met when they were five.'

Pretty much the same age Hugo and herself had become friends. The difference being her mum had a massive crush on her dad, even back then. When people saw how happy they were together, they always assumed they were newlyweds. They were usually shocked when they found out how long her parents' history went back.

'I suppose it helps when you don't have any money worries. My dad had an accident and hasn't been able to work for the past ten years. Which meant I had to leave school and get a job at sixteen just to keep a roof over our heads.'

Adriana thought about the implication of Jessica's actions and her admiration for Jessica grew. That she had taken on such a massive responsibility was a testimony to the true depth of her character, and Adriana found herself wondering if she would have had the same strength.

'Having that much responsibility must have been tough,' Adriana said, thinking Jessica would agree with her and tell her how hard it had been.

Jessica answered without even thinking for a second. 'Not at all. I know I missed out on a lot, but I like to think it helped me become the person I am today.'

'Which is?'

'Someone that doesn't take things for granted. I know first-hand how life can change in the snap of a finger. I mean look at us. What's the chance of us meeting under different circumstances?'

And me falling for you in a big way. 'I don't know—'

'Oh come off it. Let's call a spade a spade. Our social classes rarely mix unless we're working for you.'

'Are you trying to imply I'm a snob?' Adriana didn't like where this was going. She totally understood the premise behind what Jessica was saying but that didn't mean it was true. They could have met at a yoga class for instance. Yoga wasn't only for the rich.

'No, of course I'm not. I think you're amazing. All

I'm just saying is, I don't think our paths would have crossed under normal circumstances. And we certainly wouldn't be travelling to Oz together that's for sure.'

'This hypothesis is mute really, because we'll never know what might have happened.'

'Do you believe in destiny?' Jessica suddenly asked, catching Adriana off guard.

'I haven't really given it much thought. But if I'm being honest, I like to think I'm blazing my own trail. Not following a pre-determined one.'

'Why's that? Is it because a pre-determined one means you don't really have control over your life?'

'It could be,' Adriana said truthfully. There was no reason to deny that she liked being in control of her life. Which was why her parents' insistence on her getting married grated her to the bone.

'See I'm the total opposite. I don't want to freak you out or anything, but this, us being here in this place together, feels almost like we were destined to do this.'

'Don't worry, I'm not that easily freaked out,' Adriana said, thinking how much she would have liked that to be true. But in what respect were they meant to be together. Friends? Lovers? Before she could even start to believe that Jessica had come into her life for a reason, Adriana needed to find out more about her. But it seemed that Jessica had the same idea. Before Adriana could ask her about her life, Jessica said, 'Tell me about how you grew up. I've always wondered what it must be like to grow up rich.'

The manner in which Jessica asked the question

wasn't disdainful in the way it might be from someone who thought rich people were the scum of the earth. And yes, Adriana had read posts on internet forums from people who actually thought that way. They didn't realise how wrong they were. As far as she could tell there were undesirables in every community, rich and poor. Money didn't make a person nasty—they had to have that seed in them to begin with.

'Well it was great, I suppose, but then I've never known any different,' Adriana said, glancing down at Jessica's empty bottle of wine and glass. She unscrewed the lid off the water bottle, poured it into a plastic cup and gave it to her to drink.

'I don't want water, thanks,' Jessica slurred as her head bobbed slightly. 'I'm gonna get some more wine.'

'I'd drink some water first. We've got a long way to go yet.'

'Okay, Mum.' Jessica put the cup to her mouth and drank the lot in one go. 'That's better. Maybe you're right. I should slow down.'

'Do you want a coffee?'

'I think I'd better.'

Adriana pressed the assistance button and when the hostess came, she asked for two coffees. She put milk in her own but gave Jessica hers black.

'Did you travel a lot when you were younger?' Jessica said, between sips of her drink.

'Yes,' she said smiling at the memory. 'My grandmother bought a ski lodge in the Swiss Alps. I always go there on holiday when time permits.'

'I suppose that's where you'll take your husband and—'

'Husband?'

'I assume you'll get married at some stage. Knock out a few kids to carry on the family genes so to speak.'

Adriana was astonished that Jessica even had an inkling of what she was up against, even if she had only said it in jest. Pride or the thought of being a stereotype—the rich marrying the rich—stopped her from admitting Jessica was spot on. 'Hmm, I don't know about that.'

'Which one? The children or the husband?'

'Either.' Adriana took a sip of water, more as a distraction than a need for a drink. 'So what about you?'

'What about me?'

'Are you seeing someone?' Adriana asked, hoping to take the spotlight off herself.

'I wish I was, even if it was for a quick shag,' Jessica blurted out then just as quickly slammed her hand over her mouth. 'Oops sorry. Too much information there.'

Adriana laughed. 'I don't think anyone heard you.'

'But you did.'

'Is that a problem?'

'Well no but.' She paused.

'But what?' Adrianna pressed.

'I don't want you thinking ….'

Adrianna raised her eyebrows. 'Thinking?'

Jessica gave a self-depreciating laugh. 'That I'm a sex-starved lesbian.'

Adriana felt a swoosh of adrenaline hit her with

full force. *Did I just hear right? Did she just admit she's a lesbian?* 'And are you?'

'Am I what?'

'A sex-starved lesbian?'

'A lesbian, yes. Sex-starved ….' Jessica gave a nervous laugh as she flicked her hair over her shoulder. 'No.'

Her mouth suddenly dry, Adriana took another sip of water. She couldn't help wondering if Jessica could sense her excitement at this unexpected news. 'So it's not a problem then, is it?'

At that moment, an air hostess appeared at her side bringing their conversation to an abrupt end. 'Another drink, madam?'

'I think I need a bottle of wine!' Jessica said.

The hostess handed Jessica a small bottle of wine and a plastic glass. Adriana declined, instead opting to slip a Valium in her mouth. As well as settling her nerves that were now exploding in parts of her body that she didn't know existed, it would help with the cabin fever she normally suffered from long haul flights. If the situation hadn't been so urgent, Adriana would never have done the whole trip in one go. Instead, she would have had a stopover somewhere for a couple of days to break up the long journey. But finding Edwina was of the utmost importance and if she had to be inconvenienced for twenty-four hours, so be it.

They touched down in Dubai and milled around the airport for a couple of hours. Eventually they boarded the next flight and settled into their seats. They were both weary now and all Adriana wanted to do was relax.

Jessica seemed to have found a film she wanted to watch and slipped on her headphones. Relieved, Adriana brought out her book to read, picking up where she left off.

Before long, the sky outside grew dark and the cabin crew dimmed the lights. Adriana fell asleep shortly after.

When Adriana awoke with a dead arm, she found Jessica's head nestled against her shoulder, her hand carelessly resting on her knee. Carefully lifting up her arm not to disturb Jessica, she glanced at her wristwatch. She had been asleep for eight hours straight which was a first for her. For the rest of the flight Adriana watched the new releases and Jessica never woke up until they neared their destination.

When they finally touched down at Sydney airport and alighted from the plane, Jessica looked around her in wonder.

'Wow! The people here don't look any different to the people in London,' she said gesturing to the airport staff.

'You sound disappointed?'

Jessica pulled her face. 'I am a bit. I don't know why but I thought there'd be something to differentiate everyone.'

'Like?' Adriana said as they walked into the airport.

'I dunno.' Jessica shrugged.

'Well, they do have kangaroos here,' Adriana said

smiling. 'I still can't believe you nearly slept the whole way.'

Jessica grinned sheepishly. 'To be honest I'm not much of a drinker, it doesn't take a lot to knock me out.'

'I'll have to remember that.'

'Look, Adriana,' Jessica said, stopping for a moment. 'I just wanted to say sorry if I spoke out of turn on the plane.'

'Don't be silly.' Adriana gestured for them to carry on walking. 'That's the beauty of free speech. You can say what you want.'

They collected their cases from the luggage carousel and made their way to the hotel Adriana's father had booked. When the driver pulled up outside the glass fronted building situated right opposite the coastline, Adriana breathed a sigh of relief. Her father might have disappointed her by booking her into economy but the classy looking hotel was more than enough to make up for it. At the reception desk they were greeted by Mandy, who could only be described as a 'beach babe'—blonde, tanned, gleaming white teeth and a body so toned it looked like it needed twenty-four-hour maintenance. To say she wasn't slightly intimidated by this bronze goddess would have been an outright lie.

'Let's see,' Mandy said. Adriana was somewhat surprised to find out that he'd booked them a twin room. Jessica looked relieved at the news and Adriana could only put it down to Jessica's fear of sleeping alone in a foreign country. Once the porter had deposited their cases in their room, Adriana walked over to the window and drew back the curtains.

'Come take a look,' Adriana said and Jessica walked over to join her.

They were way up on the fifth floor and the reflection from the moon bounced off the dark still waters giving the scene before them a dark and eerie mood.

'Oh wow!' Jessica said. 'I've never seen anything like this before in my life.'

'It's amazing, isn't it?' Adriana said, before she turned and her eyes wandered to the two double beds separated by a side cabinet. 'Which bed do you want?'

'The one by the door, I'm a light sleeper so I'll hear if anyone tries to break in.'

'Have you got safety issues?'

'More like daddy issues.' Jessica crossed her arms over her chest. 'I think it comes from him not being able to protect us when our house got robbed.'

'Oh my God, I hope no one was hurt.'

'Nah, but the bastards did take my action man. I was gutted.'

Adriana's eyebrows shot up. 'Action man?'

'Yeah, I know, but I've always thought of Barbie as one of the mean girls. She's so perfect, always immaculately dressed and hangs out with her equally perfect friends. If she could speak, I'm sure it would be nonstop about herself and bloody Mr perfect Ken.'

Adriana laughed. 'That's why I'm glad all I had was a pony to play with. He was totally non-judgmental. Do you need to use the bathroom first?'

'I'm good thanks.'

'Help yourself to room service then.'

'Do you want anything?'

'Something smothered in chocolate.'

'Really? You don't look the type to eat junk food. I mean you're so fit looking.'

'Pilates five times a week,' Adriana said taking her toiletry bag from her case into the bathroom with her. She ran the bath and poured the Epsom salts in and undressed while it filled.

Adriana must have dozed off because when her eyes flew open in response to the urgent tapping on the door, she realized the water had cooled considerably.

'Adriana, are you okay in there?' Jessica's voice was filled with concern.

'I'm just getting out, won't be a minute,' she called back, pushing herself into a standing position. She stepped out onto the mat, reached for the hotel dressing gown and slid into it. She felt exhausted.

'I thought I was going to have to break the door down and rescue you,' Jessica said nervously. 'I wouldn't want you to drown before you have your chocolate cake and tea.'

Jessica pointed to the table that stood in front of the window.

'Mmm, looks yummy, thank you.' Adriana walked over to it and broke off a piece of cake with the edge of a fork. When the sweetness hit her taste buds she briefly closed her eyes. 'Oh, it tastes amazing, try some.'

Lips apart, Adriana spoon fed her the cake and when Jessica let out a mouth-watering groan, Adriana fought off the desire to kiss her. *Maybe she is my destiny.*

'I'm starting to feel delirious,' Adriana said, wondering why she would even think such a thing. 'I'd better get some shut eye.'

'Me too,' Jessica said. 'Do you mind if we keep the curtains open?'

'Of course not.' Adriana shrugged off her robe and slipped naked into bed.

'Sweet dreams,' Jessica said as she pulled the sheet up to her chest.

They will be if they're about you.

Chapter Ten

A sliver of moonlight shone brightly through the hotel room window, giving just enough light for Jessica to see the silhouette of Adriana's form in her bed. Minutes earlier it had afforded her a sneaky peek of Adriana's toned naked body as she disrobed before disappearing between the sheets. Jessica had instantly felt like a teenage boy seeing a naked woman for the first time. Even though ten minutes had passed, the throbbing persisted between her legs and she had no idea how to make it stop. Part of her wanted it to pass but another part liked it. For the past few months, Jessica had thought she was going to be numb from the waist down forever. All at the tender age of twenty-three.

Jessica turned onto her back, then when she couldn't get settled, rolled onto her side, then her front, then her back again. Her mind filtered between the image of Adriana's naked body and all the things she would like to do to her, and the fact that she had drunkenly spilt the beans. Had she done the right thing telling Adriana she was gay? Adriana hadn't seemed the slightest bit fazed, but then again you just didn't know how people took to finding out that you weren't straight. Some of her former 'friends' had seemed all right with it initially, only to start changing their behaviour when she was around them. Like not sharing a bed with her in their underwear after a night out or stiffening when she went to give them a hug. She only hoped things weren't going to be awkward with Adriana now that she knew the truth.

Before long Jessica's eyes closed and vivid images of Adriana played in her mind's eye as she drifted off to sleep.

When she awoke hours later, Jessica felt as if she was surrounded by a dense fog. No matter how hard she tried, she just couldn't get into the groove of things. Getting dressed took a lot of effort, as did brushing her teeth. It was as if everything she tried to do was happening in slow motion. Downstairs in the bright and airy hotel dining room, her breakfast plate remained untouched as the only things she could consume without any difficulty were copious amounts of coffee. Whether it was helping Jessica didn't know, but she was at a loss what else to do.

'You've got jet lag,' Adriana said, cutting a banana into slices. Funnily enough, Adriana didn't seem to be suffering from it. She looked radiant.

'I feel like death.' Jessica took another mouthful of coffee.

'I've got some melatonin in my case. It should help.'

'I hope so, I feel like I'm going to have a panic attack.'

Adriana closed her hand over Jessica's and for that brief moment, a spark of light was injected into Jessica's dark, gloomy world. That was until Adriana removed it and things faded back to grey.

'I promise, it'll pass. The first time I had jetlag I

had a massive panic attack.'

'Oh God, don't say that. If that happens to me, it'll finish me off. I've never felt so vulnerable and scared in my life.'

'Do you remember what I told you in London. I will not let anything happen to you. And even if you do have a panic attack, I'll be there with you. All right?'

'All right, thank you,' Jessica said, running a clammy hand through her hair.

'Did you manage to get any sleep at all?'

Jessica perked up a little as she remembered what had kept her up most of the night. Thinking about Adriana laying naked in the bed a few feet away. 'A couple of hours I think. Though I can't be sure. I don't know what feels real and what doesn't at the moment.'

'Try and eat something. And drink lots of water. You're probably still dehydrated as well.'

Jessica's shoulders slumped. Why hadn't she listened to Adriana when she had tried to make her drink a bottle of water in the middle of the night. She had refused because she didn't want to be up and down peeing all the time. As they sat there and despite how dreadful she felt,
Jessica decided she wouldn't want to be anywhere else in the world at that moment.

She even found herself secretly hoping that her nan had left Sydney, as that would mean they'd have to stay longer in order to find her. She didn't want to go back to the UK. Not yet. Even though it was important to get her hands on the £100,000 as soon as possible, an extra few days wouldn't hurt. Besides, the sooner the trip ended the sooner Jessica would be hurtled back into her mundane existence and that was the last thing she wanted.

'I think you should go back up to our room and take it easy for a while. If you feel better this afternoon, we can drive over to your grandmother's hotel,' Adriana suggested.

'Sounds like a plan.' Jessica was glad to see Adriana wasn't pissed off with her for ruining their first day in Sydney.

'Good. Go up then and I'll use the hotel's computer to find the address.'

'Cool,' Jessica said warily pushing herself to her feet. All she could think about now was sleep. Nothing else mattered. Not her nan. Not the money. Nothing.

When she woke, in what felt like hours later, the room was basked in a warm golden glow and this instantly reinvigorated her. Her arms and legs in a long lazy stretch, Jessica opened her eyes and jerked back slightly when she saw Adriana sitting on the edge of her bed, staring at her. Adriana had changed out of the shirt she wore earlier and was now wearing a silky vest. When Adriana moved forward slightly, Jessica could see the swell of her breasts. It was the perfect view to wake up to.

'Oh God, please don't tell me I've been dribbling?' Jessica said swiping her hand over her mouth. She could think of nothing more embarrassing if she had. Other than talking dirty in her sleep that is.

'No,' Adriana said softly. 'You looked so peaceful.'

'Really?' Jessica said wondering what Adriana's interpretation of peaceful was.

'Yes. Are you feeling better?'

'Loads.' Jessica propped her head up on a pillow. 'So did you find the guesthouse?'

'Guesthouses you mean. Apparently, the Soft Rainbow is a chain, you must have called their head office from London and not the actual guesthouse. There are over ten —'

'Ten?'

'Yes, maybe we should have done a little bit of research before we left London,' Adriana said with a wry smile. 'Anyway, I've hired a car as many of them are in the suburbs. So when you're ready….'

It didn't take Jessica long to shower and dress and soon they were out in the Australian heat, walking across the road from their hotel in Darling Harbour to the car Adriana had rented. Jessica was relieved the car had air conditioning as the heat blasting through the passenger side window felt like a furnace on her face.

Adriana tapped the address in the GPS for the nearest Soft Rainbow guesthouse then turned towards Jessica with a mega-watt smile. 'Ready?'

Thankfully Adriana's eyes were hidden behind sunglasses. Although Jessica was getting used to them, they still had an intense effect on her. 'Sure am.'

As the car moved off, Jessica scanned the radio until she found a channel that was playing hits from the 90s, and soon they were both humming along to the tunes.

Being with Adriana was like hanging out with your best friend or your sister. There was a kind of familiarity between them that made Jessica feel as if she had known her a lifetime.

'Just out of curiosity,' Adriana said, 'is your grandad still alive?'

Funnily enough, Jessica was just thinking about her grandad and how sad it was that he had died without having the opportunity to travel and see the world. 'No, he had a heart attack years ago.'

'Did Edwina remarry?'

'Nope. Thinking about it, I'm not sure she even dated after he died.'

'She must have been lonely.'

'I don't know about that. My nan's always been an independent sort. And to be honest, I think my grandad pissed her off to no end. And when he retired things got worse. I don't think she liked him being at home all day pottering around. She enjoyed her own company too much.'

'Retirement seems to do that to a lot of relationships,' Adriana said reflectively. 'By the way, do you have a photograph of your grandmother—'

'I sure do.' Jessica fished her phone out of her pocket and brought up a picture of Edwina. Her silver hair was short and flat against her head and Jessica noticed for the first time that the big smile on her face somehow didn't filter through to her eyes. Had she actually misjudged her nan's situation? That she was lonely? No, she couldn't have. Surely her parents would have said something. Or at the very least made an effort to have her over more often.

Adriana took a quick glance at the photo. 'I can see where you get your good looks from. I'm sure no one will ever forget your grandmother after seeing that beautiful face.'

Jessica felt her cheeks heat up despite the cool air. Since they'd arrived in Sydney, she thought Adriana was being, not flirty exactly, but more relaxed. Open with her. Not guarded in the way she had been in London. It was like being with another woman. And it was because of Jessica not wanting to spoil the atmosphere that she hadn't probed any further into Adriana's personal life. It was odd, Jessica thought, that Adriana seemed to hate talking about herself. Most people she knew wouldn't do anything but. And while Jessica liked that quality about her, it also meant that she was no closer to finding out whether Adriana was into women or not.

Jessica gazed out of the window as they drove through the city. She couldn't take it all in, couldn't believe she was actually there. As they approached the Sydney Harbour Bridge, Jessica gasped.

'What's wrong?' Adriana asked, concern etched on her face.

'Oh nothing, sorry. It's just I've seen the bridge on TV but never expected to actually drive over it, ever.'

Adriana laughed. 'We can climb it if you want? It has beautiful views from the top of the opera house.'

'Are you kidding? Have you seen how high it is?'

Adriana rolled her eyes. 'You only live once.'

Jessica smiled. 'You only die once too.'

As they headed north, the high-rise buildings and busy streets gave way to parks and houses. Eventually the sat-nav indicated that they were only minutes away from their destination. They pulled into a quiet road lined with boarded up store fronts. Several men hung around on the street corner talking to one another.

Jessica's senses heightened. *What if we get mugged?*

Stop it, she told herself angrily. *For one day just give your crime-ridden brain a rest.* Hadn't Ariel warned her about watching nothing but crime TV? That it would warp her mind and sense of reality? Yes, she had, but that didn't mean Jessica had listened to her. It was like going cold turkey watching 'happy' programs. Real life just wasn't like that, where everyone had 'flat line' days and nothing ever happened. *Nothing!* Where there was no drama. No discord amongst family and friends. In other words, normal TV was unrealistic.

Up ahead in the distance, Jessica noticed what looked like a large disjointed building. The multi-coloured Soft Rainbow sign was discoloured and peeling. Car tyres, old bicycles and motorbikes were littered around. She silently prayed that her nan had more sense than to book into such a place. It gave her the willies just looking at it. Adriana slowed the car and pulled up outside.

'What an eyesore.' Adriana removed her glasses and peered up at the building.

'That's putting it kindly.'

Adriana looked at her. 'What do you think? Is it even worth checking out?'

'I think we should, 'cause if my nan is in there I'll be taking her straight out,' Jessica said.

They both stepped out of the car simultaneously and the heat smothered them. Reaching back in the car Jessica took out her bottle of water and swallowed a mouthful. She offered it to Adriana who shook her head. *She's like a cactus.* It was the only explanation as Jessica couldn't fathom why the heat didn't seem to faze Adriana in the slightest.

They made their way up the creaky wooden staircase and gingerly pulled open a glass door that was hanging off its hinges. A thin wiry man sat in a chair at the side of a small desk. Jessica couldn't believe her eyes. There wasn't any air conditioning in the space but the man had on a thick black jumper. Just looking at him made her feel claustrophobic.

He stood as they neared his desk.

'Hi.' Adriana held out her hand and he shook it. 'I wonder if you could help us, we're looking for ….'

Jessica handed Adriana her phone with the photo of her nan still on the screen.

'…. Edwina Wilson. She might be staying here.'

The man's eyes remained trained on Adriana's face. 'You sound like you're a long way from home.'

There was something in the way he said it that made the hairs on the back of Jessica's neck stand up to attention. She had watched far too many Australian crime shows to know that if he killed them he could dispose of their bodies in the outback and no one would find them for years, if at all.

'No, not really.' Jessica's voice shook. 'We live in, um, the centre of Sydney and our husbands are just down the road taking pictures.'

He narrowed his eyes. 'Pictures of what? There aren't many tourist attractions round here, mate.'

'You know what policemen are like. They always find something to investigate.'

He took a step forward. 'So your husband's a policeman? What about yours?' he asked, turning abruptly to Adriana.

Jessica nudged her.

'Oh my husband, he's very high up in the police force. He's a commissioner.'

He wiped his hand vigorously on the thigh of his sweat-sodden jeans. 'Is that right?'

'Yes, look have you seen this woman or not?'

Jessica was impressed by Adriana's confidence and she could only put it down to ignorance. How Adriana wasn't getting the menacing vibe from the man was beyond her.

For the first time, he looked down at the picture and slowly shook his head. 'Can't say I have and I'm not allowed to give out guest information anyway. Privacy and all.'

This time Jessica held out her hand to him, in the hope if he felt how strong her handshake was, he might think twice about attacking them. She wasn't taking any chances of being murdered on her first day and being left in the outback to be eaten by dingoes.

'Oh well not to worry.'

He kept hold of her hand. 'I can see you've got the same eyes.'

'Yeah, that's what everyone says.' Jessica snatched her hand back, grabbed Adriana by the elbow and pulled her towards the door.

'Thanks for your help,' Jessica called out as they backed out of the room, and arm in arm ran down the stairs laughing.

'What was that about?' Adriana asked once they were back in the car.

'I can't believe you even have to ask. That man had "serial killer" written all over his face. If we can't find my nan, I know exactly who to point the finger at.'

Adriana laughed. 'Come on, he wasn't that bad.'

'Oh really? Didn't you see the way he was looking at you? As if he could just picture you—'

'All right. I get the idea.' Adriana started the car and manoeuvred it back onto the road.

'When we stop at the next place, one of us goes into the reception and the other stands at the exit holding the door open. Agreed?' Jessica said.

'If it makes you feel better, agreed.'

'Good. So how far is the next one?'

'According to my map, it's a few miles ahead.'

The next Soft Rainbow guesthouse was what Jessica had expected all along. It was a picturesque dwelling with a small landscaped garden surrounded by blooming flowers. It looked just the kind of place her nan would like staying at. And when Jessica met Bea, the manager, she felt a glimmer of hope and sadness. Hope that her nan would be there and she'd get to see her and sadness that this could be the end of their travels.

'What a lovely looking lady,' Bea said gazing down at the picture of her nan.

'Yes, she is,' Jessica said. Even though Bea wasn't as scary as the last guesthouse manager, she still made Adriana keep watch at the entrance. She couldn't be too trusting. 'Have you seen her by any chance?'

'I'm afraid not dear, we've only just opened the doors today. The place has been refurbished,' Bea said. 'I must say, it's nice to hear a British accent again. I went to England once.'

'Oh that's good, anywhere nice?' Jessica said, not wanting to be rude and just take off.

'Manchester. Do you know it?'

'Yes, but I've never been before.'

'I don't blame you.' Bea rolled her eyes. 'It did nothing but rain the whole time I was there.'

'Yeah, I've heard people say that,' Jessica said. It was one of the reasons she had never ventured there. The weather was bad enough in London. 'Well thanks for your time.'

'I hope you find your grandma.'

'Me too.'

'No luck?' Adriana said as they walked back to the car.

'Nope. You didn't think it was going to be this easy, did you?'

'A girl can dream, can't she?'

'You never know, she might be at the next place.'

Adriana and Jessica kept on with their search, stopping at each of the guesthouses on the list, asking guests and staff, but no one remembered seeing Edwina.

Minutes turned into hours and despite stopping for a sandwich for lunch Jessica's stomach rumbled, giving the impression she hadn't eaten for days.

'Maybe we should head back to our hotel before it gets much darker,' Jessica suggested.

'At least we've made some progress today. Although they couldn't tell us much, I'm pretty certain your grandmother hadn't stayed at any of those places,' Adriana said, turning the car round and heading back in the direction of their hotel. 'She must have checked into one of the guesthouses just outside of Sydney. We'll check them out tomorrow.'

When they got to their room, Adriana and Jessica flopped onto their beds.

'Hungry?' Adriana asked as she kicked off her shoes.

'Starving.'

'Can you be bothered to eat downstairs?' Adriana reached for the menu on the cabinet. 'Shall we order room service?'

'Sounds like a plan. But I need to take a quick shower. I feel grimy,' Jessica said rolling off the side of her bed.

'What do you fancy?' Adriana asked, smothering a

yawn with her hand.

Apart from taking you in my arms and ravishing you? 'I'm easy. You choose,' Jessica said before disappearing behind the bathroom door.

The hot spray of water washed away the grime and sweat that had accumulated on her skin. Jessica smiled to herself, thinking of the great day she'd had. It had been like a mini adventure. Driving to different places and meeting so many nice people, bar the creepy man at the beginning, had been fun. And though a fire hadn't been lit between Adriana and herself *yet*, there was something definitely simmering beneath the surface. Jessica could just sense it.

Feeling refreshed and a lot hungrier than she realised, Jessica's eyes widened when she exited the bathroom and saw the tray on her bed with a burger the size of the Eiffel tower sat in the centre. How she was going to fit her mouth around it, Jessica didn't know, but she was going to die trying.

'How is it?' Adriana asked as Jessica opened her mouth as wide as possible and took a quick bite. She only managed to grab the excess burger and cheese that oozed outside the bun, but at least she'd got some of it.

When her mouth was empty, she said, 'Tasty, pity I can't get my whole gob around it.'

'The name should have given it away. Oz's tower. But to be honest, I didn't think they meant literally.'

'It's all right,' Jessica said going in for a second bite. 'Though I'll probably still be chewing on it come midnight.'

'Do you want some of my salad?' Adriana held out her plate and Jessica shook her head. There was nothing more boring than salad and she didn't care who disagreed with her. Not to mention the astronomical prices restaurants charged for plating up limp salad leaves and a bit of tomato, cucumber and red onion as if it were a masterpiece. No, Jessica would stick with her burger even if it did clog her arteries. At least she'd die happy. *And more important than anything—die feeling full.*

Using her knife, Jessica sliced the burger into manageable pieces and in no time at all the burger was gone. Looking over at Adriana still picking at her salad, Jessica said, 'We should have shared my burger.'

Adriana glanced over at her. 'I don't eat meat.'

'Oh, shit, sorry.' Jessica quickly covered her plate with her napkin in the hope of hiding the remaining crumbs of the burger bun. 'I hope I haven't put you off your food.'

Adriana waved away her concern with her hand. 'Not at all, I'm just not very hungry.'

'Must have been those two Nutella crepes you had for lunch.'

'Maybe,' Adriana said smiling.

Seemingly giving up on her salad, Adriana put her plate on the side and curled up into a ball, facing Jessica as she absent-mindedly chewed on her remaining French fries.

'Do you want to watch a movie?' Adriana said.

'Uh huh,' Jessica replied, relieved Adriana didn't want an early night.

'Have you seen IT before?'

Jessica let out a nervous breath and shook her head. 'I don't do horror films. Especially ones with clowns. I'm scared shitless of them.'

Adriana gave her an appraising look. 'Really? How come?'

'Oh, you don't want to know.' Jessica felt a rush of embarrassment and wished she hadn't said a word.

'Yes I do. Tell me.'

Jessica smiled ruefully. 'All right. But swear you won't laugh.'

'I swear,' Adriana said, putting her hand against her chest.

Jessica rubbed her face. She'd never told anyone before because she knew how stupid it was to be a grown woman with an irrational fear of clowns, but it had been that way for years. 'Okay, when I was twelve I watched a film called Killer Klowns from Outer Space.'

Jessica didn't miss the smirk Adriana tried to hide behind her hand but she carried on regardless. 'I'd already been traumatised by the clown in Poltergeist, so watching that film straight after made me believe clowns were all evil.'

'Aww that's so sad,' Adriana said with genuine sympathy.

'You think?'

'Yes. Clowns were an integral part of my life until I was around thirteen. Every year my parents hired one for my birthday party.'

'Glad I didn't know you back then,' Jessica said as

a chill ran through her just thinking about coming close to a clown—evil or not.

'You know there's only one way to conquer your fears?'

'To face them?' Jessica asked cautiously. She knew that's what all the self–help books called for. Feel the fear and do it anyway. *How about not!* Where was the sense in traumatising yourself? There wasn't, yet she had noticed people actually bought in to that mantra. But not her. Yes, she would gladly acknowledge her fears but she would leave it at that.

'Exactly!' Adriana said. 'Come on, let's watch it.'

'No, seriously, you go right ahead. I'll go and read in the bath.'

'You'll do no such thing. Come on!'

Jessica's eyes grew wide as Adriana rolled onto her back and patted the now empty space beside her. 'You want me to get on your bed?'

'Yes. If you get frightened, you can squeeze my hand.'

Jessica's eyes dropped to Adriana's hand and she realised even her greatest fear couldn't compete with the opportunity to be by Adriana's side for two hours. Jessica soon forgot the thoughts she was having seconds ago.

'If you're sure,' Jessica said, trying to sound as if she wasn't too convinced the method Adriana proposed would work.

'Positive. Now come on before we miss the start.'

'Okay but be warned, I have a strong grip.'

Adriana grinned. 'I think I can handle it.'

Jessica climbed off her bed and hopped onto Adriana's. She remained in a sitting position until Adriana found the channel showing the film, then she slid down beside her and put a pillow on top of her chest.

'Do you want to hold my hand now?' Adriana asked ten minutes into the film.

As if I'm going to say no. Jessica took hold of Adriana's hand and closed her eyes, wanting to savour the moment. She must have kept them closed a lot longer than she thought because Adriana suddenly asked in a concerned voice. 'You okay, Jess?'

Adriana startled her by the shortening of her name more than anything else and she automatically pulled her hand away. The way Adriana said 'Jess' was as if they were on more intimate terms than they really were.

Jessica opened her eyes and looked straight into Adriana's. The nerve endings throughout her entire body prickled and tingled. It would be so easy to lift her neck just a little off the pillow and in seconds her lips would be pressed against Adriana's. But how long would it be before Adriana either slapped her and threw her off the bed, or worse, out of the hotel room?

Jessica knew the fantasy she had in her head about them getting down and dirty, wasn't going to happen. Not in this lifetime anyway. They lived in different worlds. Not that Jessica wouldn't jump at the chance of stepping up on the social ladder, but she doubted very much Adriana would want to step down and enter her world with the same enthusiasm. So no, Jessica wouldn't make a move on Adriana, she would keep her thoughts to herself and when the trip was over, she would live with the memory of what could have been the best romance of her life.

'Yeah, I'm fine.'

'Do you want me to turn it off?'

'No, it's all right, I—'

'Come on.' Adriana turned on her side and with her right hand reached back for Jessica's again. 'Cuddle up, I think it's going to get scary from here.'

Jessica let her hand slide over Adriana's rib cage and rest lightly against her stomach as she shuffled closer to spoon Adriana's body. She no longer cared about the stupid clown on TV acting menacingly towards a young boy. There were only two thoughts going around in her mind. One was whether or not her heart could actually explode at the rate it was beating. And two—could Adriana feel it pumping against her back. Because if she could, she wasn't letting on. Jessica let her head sink into the pillow and closed her eyes again as she felt herself floating with euphoria. *Maybe I should tell her I have a fear of sleeping alone. And with my clothes on.* She grinned at this thought, wondering if Adriana's body was as smooth and silky as her hand. If her breasts were as firm as they'd looked when she caught sight of her naked the night before.

Hmm. Jessica licked her lips as a vivid image of Adriana slipping between the sheets popped up in her mind's eye. Only it wasn't her own bed she was getting into, it was Jessica's. And she was pulling Jessica into her arms, their bodies moulding as one when Jessica sank against her, feeling the contours of Adriana's body. Adriana's nipples, hard against her own. And then her mouth finding Adriana's and unsurprisingly they fit perfectly. 'I want you so much.'

'Sorry, I didn't catch what you said.'

Adriana's voice brought Jessica's thoughts to a screeching halt and she came hurtling back to reality with a disappointing thud. It had felt so real. So right.

'I didn't say anything,' Jessica said quickly as she pulled her hand back and pushed herself into a sitting position. 'I must have dozed off.'

Adriana twisted around to look at her. 'You do look tired. Shall we call it a night?'

'Yeah. Although you don't have to turn the TV off.'

'Probably best if I get some shut eye too. See you in the morning.'

'That you will,' Jessica said getting back into her own bed.

The fact that Adriana knew Jessica was gay and still let her get into bed with her spoke volumes. Either Adriana was just a warm, friendly person who didn't mind getting up close and personal with other women, or she was gay.

Jessica dared to dream it was the latter.

Chapter Eleven

Early the next morning, Adriana was woken by the mesmerising sound of waves lapping the embankment outside their window. Stretching, she glanced over at Jessica who was still dead to the world. Her left arm and leg draped loosely over her pillow as if she was holding a lover. *She looks so cute.* Adriana's eyes dropped to Jessica's slightly pouting mouth and she fought the irrational desire to reach over and plant a kiss on them. The fact that kissing Jessica would feel so natural made Adriana think about the life that awaited her back in the UK. Would she be able to do it? Marry Hugo despite not feeling the slightest bit attracted to him. Or could she find the courage to go against her parents' wishes and blaze her own trail and live the life she wanted?

It frustrated her that her father had homed in on Hugo, of all people, for her to marry. Friends since five, she had never actually told Hugo she was gay. Maybe if she had it would have put a stop to him showering her with expensive gifts, which she always returned, or late night phone calls, which she always ignored.

Thoughts flowed. Mainly ones of guilt. No matter which way she turned, someone was going to get hurt. Maybe once she had her inheritance, she could sail off in to the horizon with the woman she loved. For some unknown reason, Adriana turned her head to look at

Jessica when she thought this. *Don't be so silly*, she told herself for even considering such a thought, *we have nothing in common*. Though this might be true, it didn't mean Adriana hadn't enjoyed Jessica's company, because she had. In fact, the more time Adriana spent with her the more she realised she was going to miss her once their journey ended.

For the first time that morning, Adriana thought about her grandmother's letter that was safely in her bag. As always, it made her wonder what was so important that her grandmother had withheld her inheritance. She knew it would leave Adriana in a bind, so for her to do that meant it was something that was very close to her heart. But what? She had a vision of herself finding Edwina and handing it over, only to discover that it was something so totally irrelevant it wouldn't have mattered if it found its way into Edwina's hands. *No*, Adriana immediately disregarded the thought. If it was one thing her grandmother didn't do, it was waste time. To her, every moment of life was precious and she would not send Adriana on a wild goose chase if it wasn't something she needed her to do.

Adriana heard, rather than saw, Jessica stir and let out a long groan. Wriggling her fingers in the air, Jessica looked over at Adriana with a sleepy smile. A strand of tousled hair fell across her eye.

'Morning,' Jessica said.

God she's so sexy. 'Good morning, did you sleep well?'

'Like a baby. What time is it?'

'I don't know.' Adriana leant over and grabbed her phone from the bedside cabinet. There were several messages from Alice and a few friends. The last one was from Hugo. Seeing the first line of his text made her stomach sink. No doubt her parents had told him she'd gone slinking off to Australia in search of the mysterious woman who held the key to her inheritance. Without even opening the text, she knew what the gist of his message would be. He'd want to know why she hadn't asked him to go with her in his dad's private plane no doubt. She deleted the message without reading it. 'Eight o'clock.'

'Feels a lot later.'

'You feeling better today?'

'Much.' Jessica lifted her head gently and glanced towards the window.

'Good.' Unable to bare the torment of looking at Jessica and not being able to reach over and touch her, Adriana decided to put some distance between them. 'Do you want to use the bathroom first?'

'Sure.' Jessica rolled out of bed. 'Won't be a min.'

When Adriana flopped her head back on the pillow and heard the sound of the shower minutes later, her mind inadvertently wandered to thoughts of what Jessica was doing right at that moment. Was she washing her hair with the shampoo that smelt of coconuts? Or soaping herself with the lavender body wash? Were her hands roaming slowly over her soapy breasts? Down her stomach? Between her legs?

Adriana gave herself a mental shake. She shouldn't

be thinking about Jessica in this manner. Not when her personal life was such a roller coaster. But she was finding it more and more difficult to control her emotions as each day passed. Adriana didn't know why, but what she felt for Jessica was more than just a run-of-the-mill attraction. If it hadn't been, she would have probably slept with her already. Adriana squeezed her eyes shut and let her imagination run wild, telling herself there was nothing wrong with fantasising.

The heat outside was intense as they set out later that morning, the air still. The air conditioning in the car once again proved to be a saviour as they went in search of Edwina, only this time they travelled in the opposite direction to the way they had the previous day. Beside her, Jessica already turning a golden bronze, ticked off the guesthouses they'd stopped at. After their seventh stop they were still no closer to finding the elusive Edwina Wilson. It was nearing dark when they reached the last Soft Rainbow guesthouse on the list. The beautiful white cladded building with arched windows sat at the top of a hill overlooking the vast ocean. Walking side by side, they made their way to the front door in silent awe, both taken in by nature's beauty.

Jessica rang the bell and they waited a few moments before a flushed-faced, middle-aged woman opened the door.

'G'day.' She greeted them both with a warm, wide smile.

'Hi.' Jessica held out her hand which the woman shook without hesitation. 'I'm looking for my nan,

Edwina Wilson. Is she one of your guests by any chance?'

Adriana let out a silent sigh, as she prepared for the woman to say no. That she was sorry and they should perhaps try the guesthouses in the city. If Adriana heard one more person say they hadn't seen Edwina, she would literally scream at the top of her lungs.

When Jessica held out her phone for the woman to look at, Adriana half turned to start making her way back to her car, but the hesitation in the woman's voice stopped her in her tracks.

'Erm, well I'm not really supposed to give out information about our guests. She's your grandma you say?'

'Yes, and I need to find her urgently. She's been here, hasn't she? I can tell.'

The woman lowered her voice and glanced around. 'Okay, but please don't let anyone know I told you. Yes, I know Edwina. Lovely lady.'

Jessica smiled. 'Thank God.'

'Of course, I remember now, you must be Jessica. You're the apple of your grandma's eye,' she went on without taking a breath. 'We were just talking about you yesterday—'

'She was here yesterday?' Adriana suddenly blurted out, no longer able to maintain her politeness and let the woman talk uninterrupted.

'Why yes, she left late yesterday morning.'

Acknowledging that she would look insane if she

jumped up and down on the spot screaming with joy, Adriana remained still and poised. They were so close now. She could feel it in her bones. Adriana stepped forward and when she spoke there was excitement in her voice. 'Do you know where she's gone?'

'Not exactly.' The woman tapped her chin with the tip of her finger. 'But hold on a minute. She left something behind. I was going to bin it but for some reason thought I'd better hang onto it.'

The woman stepped back into her house and disappeared through another set of doors. Adriana and Jessica looked at each other questioningly.

'I can't believe we missed her. If only we would have headed south instead of north yesterday, we would have found her,' Jessica said.

'Everything happens for a reason,' Adriana found herself saying without really thinking.

'Here it is.' The woman's voice interrupted any further thoughts. Coming back to the door, she waved a piece of paper, which she handed to Jessica.

'Thank you,' Jessica said.

'When you find Edwina, tell her I look forward to seeing her again soon.'

'I will,' Jessica said returning the woman's smile.

Back in the car, Adriana switched on the light as Jessica unfolded the white sheet of paper. Both sets of eyes examined the small writing that was barely legible.

'It's a list of guesthouses.' A melancholy frown flittered across Jessica's features. 'But where are they?'

Adriana fished out her phone from her pocket.

'Only one way to find out.'

Adriana google searched the first two names on the list Jessica spelt out to her. She let out an audible sigh when she saw they were in Newcastle, a town over seventy miles away.

Which would have been fine had the sky still been a pale blue. Unfortunately, darkness was closing in on them and the distance was too far to travel. Especially on a whim which might lead nowhere.

'Why do you think Edwina left the list behind?'

Jessica shrugged. 'I have no idea. Maybe it's because she doesn't need it anymore. Which means we're at a dead end.'

Adriana tilted Jessica's chin up. 'Don't be so negative. The list has to be a step in the right direction.'

'How do you figure that out?' Jessica said softly.

Recognising the intimate atmosphere between them now, Adriana retracted her hand and turned to look ahead. 'Because it shows she's still not that far in front. For all we know she could have another copy of the list.'

'And?' Jessica pressed.

Adriana turned the key in the ignition. 'And if we leave early tomorrow, there's still a good chance we can catch up with her.'

Jessica cocked her head to the side as if weighing up her argument. 'That's true.'

'But if Edwina isn't staying at any of the guesthouses, we might as well admit defeat and go home.' Adriana's voice lowered as she thought about the consequences of a failed trip. Not only would she not get her inheritance in time to buy Beatrice's apartment, but she would have also let both Beatrice and Edwina down by not delivering the letter.

Adriana should have anticipated how difficult the task of finding Edwina would be. And if her decision had been made from her mind not her heart, she would have. But it had been through sheer desperation on her part that she had been driven to travel half way across the world to put the letter into Edwina's hands. *A letter with contents I know nothing about.*

Not that their journey was all doom and gloom. There had been certain benefits, namely spending time with Jessica. She had actually underestimated how much she would enjoy being with her. When Jessica suddenly placed her hand over Adriana's knee, the heat seemed to burn through the linen material of her trousers. Her subtle touch communicated support more than anything untoward.

'It would be a shame to leave so soon, wouldn't it?'

'Yes.'

The currents in the air suddenly changed. A frisson of awareness invaded Adriana's body as she tried to push aside the sensual images that being so close to Jessica invoked, but it was pointless trying. An invisible force urged Adriana to do something. *Anything*, to step over the imaginary boundary that stood between them.

Most of Adriana's resistance was there because she didn't want to hurt Jessica. From what she'd gathered in this short time she'd known her, Jessica didn't seem the type to delve in to a fling light heartedly.

Or maybe I'm wrong and Jessica would welcome a one night stand with open arms. Maybe, just maybe, it's me that has a problem with it.

There was only one way Adriana was going to find out.

***

Back at their hotel, the blonde receptionist informed them a table was available for dining in the popular seafood restaurant, so they opted to eat there instead of their hotel room. A decision Adriana was glad they'd made, as this way she could occupy her mind with thoughts that didn't centre around Jessica and the sad fact that they might be parting company soon.

The restaurant's tables were lit with candles and soft low lighting lent an air of romance to their surroundings. Classical music played along in the background adding to the serene atmosphere. A glass of red wine was just what Adriana had needed to relax and put her worries on the back burner.

'Aren't oysters meant to make you horny or something?' Jessica's mouth lifted into a small mischievous grin as she added salt and lemon juice to the oyster she held in her hand.

'You tell me?' Adriana watched in amusement as red coloured Jessica's cheeks.

'Oh um.' Jessica swallowed the oyster before reaching for her wine glass. 'I've had way too many of these.'

'It's only your second one,' Adriana reminded her.

'Is it?' Jessica gave a slight tilt of her head, looking down at her glass as if it was the first time she had seen it. 'I could have sworn blind I'd had a few. I feel ....'

'You feel?' Adriana's eyes dropped to Jessica's mouth and lingered there.

'A bit warm.' She glanced beyond Adriana momentarily. 'And fidgety.'

Adriana looked up and wiggled her eyebrows. 'Maybe the oysters are starting to work.'

'You think?' Jessica asked, grinning from ear to ear.

Adriana nodded. They were definitely doing something to her.

'In that case, what a waste,' Jessica said in a way that made Adriana think that it really was the alcohol responsible for loosening her tongue.

'It doesn't have to be.'

Jessica tilted her head slightly and exhaled. 'Really? So where am I going to find a randy lesbian at this time of night?'

'Right here.' Adriana flashed her a smouldering look that caused Jessica to splutter out her drink.

'You!?'

'I ate oysters as well, didn't I?'

The atmosphere between them suddenly turned electric. Adriana wanted to grab her, kiss her, take her back to the hotel room and do all the things she had dreamt of doing since they first met.

A bubble of laughter suddenly burst out of Jessica's mouth. 'Quit teasing. You might be horny but you're not a lesbian.'

'And just exactly how do you know what I am?' Adriana no longer cared to keep the truth from Jessica. What was the point? It wasn't like they were going to see each other again once they returned home.

'Because you would have told me.' Jessica stared back at her in an intense way, as if she was trying to work her out.

'Why? For what reason?' Adriana batted the question straight back into Jessica's court.

'You just would have.'

Adriana felt that Jessica was holding her breath, waiting for Adriana to convince her with something stronger than a simple admission. Over the years, Adriana hadn't actually told anyone she was gay. Not verbally anyway. How things normally went down were quite simple. She liked a woman. The woman liked her back. They had sex. End of. There was never a discussion, no endless questions or coming out stories. It was what it was.

'So are you like, gay.' Jessica regarded her with sombre curiosity. 'Or bisexual?'

'Does it matter?'

'Of course it does.'

'Why?'

'Because ….'

Adriana looked at her questioningly. She was so beyond labels and what it meant to be gay, lesbian or whatever other name communities wanted to group under. She was just herself, trying to make her way unscathed in this crazy world. She didn't need to label herself to feel like she belonged somewhere. Adriana knew who she was and that was all that mattered.

'I don't know why,' Jessica continued, 'but it just does. In the same way that you've probably never been in a relationship with a poor person before.'

'I wondered when we were going to get back on that subject. Let me say this clearly, so there's no room for any doubt. I am not attracted to people because of the size of their bank account.'

Jessica's face formed an expression that told Adriana she didn't believe a word Adriana had just said. 'So you're saying you could be with a … how can I put this? An underprivileged person?'

'Yes I could. And I would, if I loved them.'

Jessica tutted, her gaze dropping to her glass. 'I can't believe you're only telling me this now.'

'Like I said, I didn't see any reason to.'

'But don't you know it's just a done thing? Look,' Jessica's head snapped up as she said assertively, 'I tell you I'm gay, like I did on the plane, then you're supposed to fess up too. See?'

'Fess up?'

'You know what I mean.' Jessica hesitated, measuring her for a moment. 'You tell me you are too. So we both know we're batting for the same side.'

'In my circle of friends, we don't discuss things that way.'

'I find that a bit strange considering you think the best policy is to be upfront and honest.'

A slight smile touched Adriana's lips as she lifted her glass to Jessica. 'Touché.'

'Do your parents know about you?' Jessica pressed on.

'No.'

'So are they expecting you to marry some rich bloke?' Jessica said with humour.

If only you knew! 'Isn't that what all parents want? For their daughters to marry well?'

The drive to push Adriana into marrying Hugo was one conversation she wouldn't be having with Jessica any time soon. The less she thought about her parents' expectations, the less real it all seemed. Especially here and now.

Jessica shook her head in disbelief. 'Jesus, this all sounds way too much like Pride and Prejudice to me. I mean we're in 2017. Isn't marrying for respectability a bit outdated now?'

'In some families,' Adriana said matter-of-factly, 'but not mine.'

'And you'd sacrifice your happiness just to make your parents happy?' Jessica said the words tentatively, as if testing her.

'Wouldn't you?'

Jessica pouted and looked thoughtful. 'I might, if we lived in a poor country and my parents needed to swap me for a goat in order to survive. But we don't. And anyway, my parents would never ask me to do something that made me unhappy.'

'So it made you happy to give up your teenage years to essentially act like an adult?'

Jessica's face flamed red and Adriana knew she'd touched a raw nerve, which hadn't been her intention. All she was trying to point out was that shit happened and people just needed to own it.

'Touché,' Jessica countered, stirring uneasily in her chair. 'The score's one, one.'

'I wasn't keeping score, I was merely pointing out the things our parents ask of us aren't always malicious, neither do they necessarily come from a bad place. My parents want what's best for me. Financial security. A roof over my head. Food on the table. Pretty much the same thing you wanted to provide for your parents, no?'

'Yeah, but I didn't have to essentially sell myself to get those things. I got a job, not a man that would expect certain things in return.'

'I take it you're talking about sex?' Adriana said nonchalantly.

'Are you effing kidding me? Of course I'm talking about sex?' Jessica leant forward, gesturing with her hands as her voice drifted into a hushed whisper. 'Sex is the most intimate thing you can do with your body. Are you really telling me you could sleep with a man even though you're into women?'

Adriana wished she knew the answer to that question. It was the one thing she didn't want to think about until she had to. Which if it was up to her parents, would be pretty soon.

'Look, my plans aren't set in stone. Who knows what's going to happen in the future,' Adriana said in the hope Jessica would leave the subject alone.

'For your sake, I hope you give it a lot more thought than you seem to have.'

'Okay, you can jump down off your soap box now,' Adriana said lightly as she stared at the woman in front of her, whose eyes blazed with passion and emotion.

Jessica tucked a stray lock of hair behind her ear and moistened her lips. 'Sorry, once I get started, I can't seem to stop.'

'That's not always such a bad thing.' Adriana glanced down and realised if Jessica moved her left hand a fraction closer their fingers would be touching, and once contact was made there would be no turning back. As she'd want even more. As if thinking along the same lines as Adriana, Jessica's eyes smouldered, heating Adriana's body in an instant.

No one had ever had such an effect on Adriana. No one.

'Do you know what I want to do?' Jessica's voice was smooth, yet oddly disconcerting.

Adriana took a long sip of wine before setting it down. 'Tell me?'

'Watch that scary clown film again.'

'Why would you want to do that if it frightens you?' Adriana said, toying with the stem of her glass. Her hand steady despite the emotional turmoil inside.

'Because I want to get into bed with you again.'

Jessica moved her seat around to Adriana's side. Her breath whispered gently over Adriana's ear as she wrapped her arm fluidly around Adriana's waist. 'Only this time I want to do more than just hold hands.'

Chapter Twelve

The hotel door had barely shut behind them, when Jessica found herself in Adriana's arms. Before she could take a breath, Adriana pressed her mouth against Jessica's parted lips, her hot, moist tongue slipping inside, seeking out Jessica's. A moan of pleasure escaped Jessica as Adriana's fingers threaded through her hair, pulling her closer as their kiss got even deeper.

Jessica's nerve endings tingled from top to bottom as Adriana pushed her back against the door and with deliberate leisure, let her hands roam down from Jessica's hair, leaving behind a scorching trail until they stopped at her breasts. Cupping them, Adriana squeezed them with just the right pressure to cause Jessica to arch to her touch, eager for more. Much, much more.

Jessica furiously tugged and pulled at Adriana's top until it loosened from her jeans. She slid her hands up Adriana's toned back, expertly releasing the clasp of her bra in a matter of seconds.

'Let me take it off,' Jessica said breathlessly between kisses. She didn't want anything between them.

Adriana silently drew back and let Jessica unbutton her shirt, all the while Adriana's gaze held Jessica prisoner. Jessica wanted, no needed to feel Adriana's hot mouth on her breasts, sucking and teasing her erect nipples, her tongue trailing down her stomach, between her thighs, to the most delicate part of her body.

Licking her, tasting her.

Jessica tugged off her own top and without giving Adriana the chance to kiss her again, she pulled Adriana's head against her chest and inhaled a short gasp when Adriana's mouth closed over her taut nipple, taking the pink bud between her teeth and nipping it gently.

Jessica fumbled with the button on Adriana's jeans, pulled it open and reached inside her underwear. Adriana's body quivered as she pushed her hand down until she found her velvet, moist centre.

'You're so wet,' Jessica mumbled, arching her head back when Adriana buried her mouth against Jessica's neck as Jessica drove her fingers into Adriana's wetness with long, slow thrusts. She withdrew only to run deliberate slow circles around Adriana's engorged centre, before driving her fingers in again. Jessica's pace built with every short gasp from Adriana, every drawn-out moan in her ear, encouraging her to thrust even harder than before.

Panting and breathless, their mouths joined again, their tongues frantic as they moved together in no particular rhythm. All that drove them was the need to be one, to touch, to feel.

Jessica, in a state of euphoria, wanted nothing more than for this moment to last forever.

'Don't you think it's time we got naked?' Adriana breathed in Jessica's ear.

Jessica didn't need to be asked twice. Her hands

tore at Adriana's clothes like a woman possessed. A woman who wanted to own every single part of Adriana's body and mind. When Adriana stood before her naked, Jessica quickly removed her own clothes, then guided Adriana towards the sofa.

Adriana smiled, giving Jessica a questioning look. 'Not the bed?'

Jessica laughed as she gently pressed Adriana down into a seated position on the two-seater sofa near the window. 'Where's the fun in that?'

The rhythmic sound of waves lapping the embankment below as a boat passed by, could be heard as Jessica lowered herself to her knees and parted Adriana's legs. Adriana took a sharp intake of breath when Jessica dropped light butterfly kisses here and there between her thighs. As she moved further along, Jessica glanced up and saw a glint of excitement in Adriana's eyes, causing her own arousal to grow. The golden glow the sunset cast over Adriana's body made the setting seem even more exotic.

It would have been near enough impossible for Jessica to want to be anywhere but here. Doing anything but this.

A tremor ran through Jessica as the tip of her tongue traced the inside of Adriana's thigh. Adriana grabbed the back of Jessica's head, slightly pushing her mouth closer to her centre. Jessica could tell by the slight twitches Adriana's legs were making that she was fighting hard to be in control. But Jessica was in charge now and she wouldn't be rushed. Not even if Adriana begged, which Jessica knew she would be by the time Jessica finished with her. When Jessica's mouth finally covered Adriana's clit, Adriana seemingly could no longer contain herself, as she writhed and bucked under Jessica's teasing tongue.

Light pressure turned firm, quick flicks turned into long deliberate strokes. Circular movements with the tip of her tongue were accompanied by short thrusts of her fingers.

Adriana's nails dug into Jessica's shoulders as she increased the pace. She knew Adriana was at her peak. The desperation for release pulsated from Adriana and Jessica finally gave in to her with a multitude of actions; probing, thrusting, licking, stroking. With Jessica's fingers still inside her, Adriana's muscles tensed, gripping them in place like a vice. Adriana covered her mouth with her hand, letting out a muffled scream as she gave herself completely to Jessica until her body went limp with exhaustion.

Jessica withdrew her fingers, reached up on her knees and fell into Adriana's open arms. Her body was clammy and hot as she pulled Jessica tight against her.

'That was amazing.'

'I aim to please,' Jessica said cockily, feeling as if she had just conquered Mount Everest without oxygen.

Adriana ran her hands over Jessica's back and Jessica shivered from the gentleness of her touch. 'Have you had much practice?' Adriana asked.

Jessica drew back to study Adriana's face. *And what a face.* If she could have bottled the sensual glow, Jessica would have been a millionaire ten times over.

'Let's just say it's been a while. I've had a lot of practice in my fantasies though.'

Adriana gave her a lazy smile. 'In that case, there's only one thing for it.'

A fresh surge of passion swept through Jessica when Adriana's hand slipped between her thighs and she arched, yearning for her. 'I'm all ears.'

'It's time,' Adriana said as she slowly stroked Jessica's centre. 'To bring your fantasies out of your head, and into reality.'

And within seconds they moved to Adriana's bed, where they remained until the early hours of the morning doing exactly that.

Chapter Thirteen

Adriana couldn't sleep. Whether it was because of the mind-blowing sex they only stopped having an hour ago, or the stress of being so close to finding Edwina only for her to slip away, she didn't know. But there was no point just lying there. With the amount of tossing and turning she was doing, it would only be a matter of time before she woke Jessica up. Taking her phone with her, Adriana went into the bathroom hoping a long hot soak would do the trick. Pouring a handful of Epsom salts onto the palm of her hand, Adriana held them under the tap until they had disappeared. As she stepped into the bath Adriana knew there was more to her agitation than finding Edwina. At the back of her mind, day and night, was the knowledge that she needed to make a decision about Hugo before she returned home. Putting it off was only making things worse for her. Could she face her fears and tell her parents she was a lesbian?

It was times like this that she wished Beatrice was still alive to guide her, as she was the only family member Adriana had confided in about her sexuality. Beatrice had also been aware of the 'plot' to get her to marry Hugo, but surprisingly she had said nothing. Which was unusual for Beatrice because she normally had a lot to say about everything, Adriana remembered fondly.

No doubt Alice had asked Beatrice not to interfere

and her grandmother had obeyed Alice's wishes. So Adriana had never asked Beatrice what to do about Hugo, thinking they would have that conversation one day. But that was the big lie life played on humans. People had a false sense of security in thinking they always had tomorrow. As Adriana had found out much too late; there was no such guarantee.

The water enshrouded Adriana's body and she dunked her head underneath it, in the hope of the silence bringing her more clarity. The transition into married life might have been easier had she not met Jessica. Her reason for this admission was simple. While her number one attraction was to women, up until now she hadn't met anyone who had blown her mind. Who had made her want to sacrifice giving up a life of security and stability.

Usually her romances were kept short and shallow. Adriana had never been in love.

Not once.

So how could she miss something that she'd never experienced? Yes, she knew sleeping with Hugo would be a massive sacrifice on her behalf, but how bad could it be? Lots of lesbians had what she termed 'convenience relationships' with men. They went in with their eyes wide open and got what they wanted out of life; children, a stable marriage and a home.

But was that really what she wanted? Even if it wasn't with Hugo, could she see herself committing to that kind of life with another woman. She searched her mind for the answer and wasn't surprised it came back with a resounding yes.

But not just with any other woman. It could only be with Jessica.

Though the realisation should have come as a surprise to her, it didn't. Deep down she had known. From the second she laid eyes on Jessica, she knew there was something special about her. That their souls somehow communicated with one another telepathically, as if they were somehow bound together from past lives.

As much as Adriana didn't want to believe in such things, there was no other explanation for it. How could it be, in a world with over six billion people, when you met 'the one' you recognised her above all others. That you just *knew*. When Adriana heard friends talk about having 'those types of feelings', it didn't make sense at the time and she had foolishly believed it never would. But meeting Jessica had changed all that.

Now she understood.

What Adriana thought she knew, and what she actually knew were two different things altogether. This was because her heart and mind spoke different languages.

Her mind made rash judgements and encouraged her to do what was right for the greater good. While her heart spoke to her tenderly and urged her to follow her instincts, to trust that whatever decision she made would be the right one.

The deciding factor for her future would come down to which voice Adriana chose to listen to.

Chapter Fourteen

The night before had been simply magical. One that Jessica would never forget. Smiling to herself, Jessica peeked at Adriana laying naked next to her for the hundredth time. The reaction was no different to the previous ones, where her heart leapt in her chest and the butterflies danced in her stomach in frenzied excitement. Every second she lay there in limbo, was every second spent not stroking Adriana's skin. Kissing her lips. Burying her face in Adriana's hair.

She wanted to do so many things, yet she couldn't bring herself to do it. Jessica didn't know the etiquette which followed a one-night stand. Did you still have free rein to touch the person you'd slept with? Or did that permission end once you both fell asleep.

Lying there now, Jessica cursed herself for not reading the article she'd come across on line about the 'dos and don'ts of a one-night stand'. She had stupidly thought it would never apply to her because she wasn't that 'type of woman'. Whoever that type of woman was. Jessica squeezed her legs together as her bladder sent an urgent message to her brain. I need to pee. *Now!* Not yet, she pleaded silently. Not until Adriana wakes.

Fate took that decision out of her hands. At that exact moment, her mobile phone started to ring. *Shit, shit, shit!* Jessica could hear it loud and clear but she was damned if she could see the sodding thing. *God knows where I left it.*

Adriana stirred as Jessica gently slid out of bed, dropped on her knees and went hunting for her phone. Sorting through their crumpled clothes strewn across the floor, she was getting nearer to the ringtone when the phone went silent. *Great!*

Finding her shirt underneath Adriana's underwear, Jessica grinned to herself then slipped into it, leaving it unbuttoned, in case she needed to remove it quickly. Levering herself up on the mattress, Jessica rested her elbows on a pillow and watched Adriana's partially covered chest as it gently rose and fell against the sheet. Just as she was about to brush a strand of hair off Adriana's cheek, her phone rang again. Jessica jerked back letting out a frustrated groan which she immediately regretted as it had been loud enough to rouse Adriana from her sleep.

'Is everything all right?' Adriana asked, rising from her pillow like a Greek goddess.

Pure perfection! 'I'm looking for my phone,' Jessica said apologetically as she pushed herself backwards and onto her feet.

'I think it's on the sofa.' Adriana's lazy smile gave Jessica a stab of longing.

'The sofa?' Jessica gulped. Dare she cast her eyes on the very place they'd made love the previous night without going blood red? 'Oh right.'

Jessica made her way to the sofa and on not immediately seeing her phone, she lifted up the cushions. She gave an awkward shake of her head when she spotted it wedged down the side. *How on earth did it get down there?*

'It's Ariel,' Jessica said when she'd retrieved it and checked the caller ID. 'Hey, how's it going?'

Jessica could hear Ariel's faint reply at the other end and just about made out what she said.

'My nan sent me a postcard?' Jessica mouthed to Adriana who was now sat upright and looking alert. She listened for a few minutes more. 'I didn't catch all of that. Listen, take a photo of it and send it to me on WhatsApp. You too, speak soon!'

Jessica made a quick dash to use the toilet as she disconnected the call. Shortly after, she returned to the room. She found the list of guesthouses in her pocket and screwed it into a tight ball. 'The list my nan left behind is useless.'

There was a shimmer of disbelief in Adriana's eyes. 'Why, what did Ariel say?'

'I think she said my nan's postcard was dated two weeks ago and that my nan said after her stay in Sydney she was going to Fiji.' She took aim at the bin and threw the paper towards it with precision. 'That's probably why she left that list behind—'

'Because she didn't need it.' Adriana cut in as if she had finally connected the dots. 'Let's just hope she's given the name of the hotel she's staying at.'

'I know it's frustrating for us, but this is great for my nan. Fiji was number one on her bucket list.' Jessica's phone bleeped in her hand and she peered down at the message from Ariel. Thankfully the writing on the back of the postcard was clear enough for her to read. 'So there's good news.'

'Go on.'

'I know where my nan's staying in Fiji.'

'Thank God for that.' Adriana swung her legs over the edge of the bed.

'I'm going to give the hotel a call. You never know, someone might actually take pity on me.'

'Yes, maybe they won't be as strict on privacy.'

Adriana's phone vibrated on the table next to her and she shot Jessica an apologetic look as she grabbed it. As soon as Adriana read her message, Jessica sensed a change in her mood almost immediately. It was as if someone else had walked into her body and replaced her. The relaxed posture she had only seconds ago was now replaced with a rigid one.

This sudden, cool, composed demeanour was a far cry from the woman that had made Jessica have six orgasms in the space of five hours. Jessica wasn't ashamed to admit that she had counted. Every. Single. One. Of. Them.

Even now, all Jessica had to do was close her eyes and she would see Adriana in the throes of passion— teeth gritted, cheeks reddened, chest rising and falling at the speed of a roller coaster and the groans, *and breathless moans*. It was enough to arouse her all over again.

'Right.' Adriana's face closed, as if guarding a secret. 'You go down for breakfast and give the hotel a call.'

Jessica's thoughts were halted by the tone of Adriana's voice. And it was because of this that she couldn't focus on Fiji or her nan's whereabouts. All she wanted to know was who had sent Adriana the message and what it had said to cause Adriana to shut down?

Was it from Adriana's parents?

Just as Jessica opened her mouth to ask, her sixth sense yelled at her not to interfere. If Adriana wanted to talk about it, she would bring it up sooner or later. So for now, Jessica would listen to her inner voice and keep her counsel.

'Do you want me to bring something back for you?' Jessica said.

'No, I'll make myself a coffee.'

'All righty, I'll get ready, then I'll be off.' Jessica backed towards the bathroom, silently praying the old Adriana would come back pretty sharpish. To say the morning after the night before had ended up like a deflated balloon would be an understatement.

Jessica's disappointment stayed with her throughout breakfast. That was until she called the hotel in Fiji who confirmed that her grandmother was staying there. Excited, she rushed back to the room.

'She's still at the hotel!' Jessica called out as she entered.

Adriana didn't look up from her phone. 'Did you speak to her?'

'No, they put me through but there was no answer. I left a message at reception for her with my number though. They wouldn't tell me how long she's staying for.'

'Okay.'

Jessica suddenly noticed the cases neatly lined up next to one another. 'I take it we're going to Fiji?' She couldn't have been gone more than twenty minutes, yet Adriana had showered, dressed and packed both their cases and managed to tidy up as well.

'Our flight to Fiji leaves at twelve,' Adriana said matter-of-factly, finally glancing up from her phone. 'I assume you want to come?'

'Just listen to the way you say that, our flight to Fiji, like we're just nipping across town, no biggie.' Adriana's aloof attitude that morning was beginning to tip Jessica over the edge. 'Do you even realise how lucky you are to be born into such a privileged family that can afford you this lifestyle?'

'I do, but I think it's a bit simplistic to think that rich people are lucky.' There was a defensive tone in Adriana's voice. Even though Jessica hadn't meant to sound critical. 'My family's wealth didn't come through luck. It came from sheer hard work.'

Adriana spoke as she wandered around the room double checking she hadn't missed anything. 'My grandfather was up at the crack of dawn and didn't finish work until long after everyone had gone home to their families. How many people around you have that sort of commitment to their work?'

Jessica thought about her job back in the UK. She knew exactly what it was like to work twelve-hour shifts and have zero family time. But that didn't make her an ambitious person. All it did was make her time poor as well as money poor.

'So you're basically saying luck has got nothing to do with your fortunes?' Jessica said sceptically. 'So if that's true, why am I struggling financially?'

Adriana's face clouded. 'I don't know, you tell me. Do you have a dream? A passion to do something so deep that it consumes your thoughts night and day.'

Apart from you? 'No I don't.'

'There's your answer,' Adriana said with a vague hint of disapproval. 'My grandfather lived for his job. He loved investment banking so much that when he lost his money in the first crash it barely took him a year to rebuild his fortune. I once read that dreams and determination are a powerful combination and it's true. So I'd be careful of passing judgement without knowing all the facts.'

'Sorry,' Jessica said accentuating the annoyance she felt with herself. She'd jumped the gun again, without giving her words much thought. From the sounds of it, Adriana's grandad was a 'self-made man' not a man whose wealth was passed down to him. When Jessica really thought about it, what pissed her off was not that certain members of society were rich, it was the way that the lesser off were treated that made her angry. That they were somehow 'less of a person', because they didn't have money or status, and as much as people liked to think that the UK was a classless society, they were living in cloud-cuckoo land.

'You don't have to apologise. I'm not implying everybody works hard for their money. I was only referring to my grandfather.'

'I know.' Disconcerted, Jessica crossed her arms and pointedly looked away.

'Anyway, let's forget about it,' Adriana said with unwelcome frankness. She grabbed the handle of her case and opened the door. 'I don't even know why this is an ongoing issue between us.'

Neither do I. It's not like we're ever going to see each other again when we get home.

They headed downstairs to a waiting taxi, all the while what Adriana had said kept bugging her. Jessica couldn't understand why she never had this elusive dream all successful people seemed to have. Of course she'd dreamt of having lots of money, a big glass house overlooking the ocean and a Porche or two. Basically all the trimmings that went with success, but she never gave thought to how she could acquire the money to pay for those things.

Jessica didn't have a particular talent. She wasn't the creative type, so she couldn't become an international bestselling author. And numbers were definitely not her strongest point, which meant any kind of high paying job that required good maths was out of the question. So what had she been put on planet earth to do? Serve food and clean up after others? Or God forbid, show her tits to a group of strangers. A sense of inadequacy swept over her and she felt a twinge of envy for those more fortunate than herself.

There has to be more to my existence than this.

Jessica was still thinking about the meaning of her life and the direction she was headed in when they arrived at the airport. Feeling nonplussed about her place in the world was a first for her. It wasn't that Jessica thought she was special, but to realise that all the future held for her was mediocrity was quite a revelation.

'You've been quiet since we left the hotel, are you all right?' Adriana asked as they stood in line to collect their tickets.

Adriana's gentle voice jolted Jessica out of her reverie. There was no point sharing her thoughts with Adriana as Jessica knew she wouldn't understand. How could a woman with the world at her feet comprehend her torment? All they shared on an equal footing was sex. Being naked was the only time neither woman could visibly show their status or wealth.

Jessica forced a smile and said, 'Nothing.'

Adriana didn't press any further, which Jessica was grateful for. Jessica stood behind her in silence as Adriana picked up their e-tickets from the machine. They were economy tickets and Jessica was slightly bemused that Adriana didn't so much as bat an eyelid. Instead, she smiled politely at the rep and simply gestured for Jessica to follow her through security, as if flying economy was the most natural thing in the world for her to do.

'Have I done something wrong?' Adriana asked.

'Wrong?'

'Yes, I feel like you're giving me the cold shoulder.'

It's not your fault being with you makes me feel like a loser.

'No. I guess I'm just tired.'

Jessica ignored the tight knot of fear in her stomach when the plane's engines roared. She tried to forget that take-off was the most dangerous part of the flight as the 400-ton metal bird sped down the runway before easing its way into the air. The plane moved from side to side, like it was balancing on a tightrope until it reached the right altitude and levelled out.

'If you're sure?' Adriana continued probing when the seat belt sign went off and Jessica let out a sigh of relief. 'Because if you want to talk about anything, I'm here.'

'Thanks, but I'm fine,' Jessica said with a ring of finality.

She swallowed the lump in her throat. The last thing she wanted to do was start blubbering like a baby because she didn't have a dream or the money to step into Adriana's world. That because of her status in life, she didn't stand a chance of winning Adriana's heart, despite what Adriana said about putting love over money.

And all because she was useless. *At everything.* Jessica struggled with the uncertainty that this knowledge aroused within her.

Adriana regarded her quizzically for a moment. 'Okay, now I know something's bothering you. What is it?'

You! Us. This. Everything. 'Noth—'

'Don't worry about it, I get it,' Adriana said dismissively. 'You're the quiet, brooding type.'

'Yeah that's what it is,' Jessica muttered. Her

misery felt like a steel weight around her neck. *Brooding! Can't she see my heart is breaking?*

Jessica slumped back in her seat and slipped the headphones over her ears. If Adriana wanted to be an insensitive cow, two could play that game.

Almost immediately Jessica felt her headphones being pulled away from her ears. She turned towards Adriana with a questioning look.

'I'm sorry,' Adriana said.

'For what?'

'For being ….' Adriana shrugged. 'Insensitive. You're upset because of what we talked about earlier, aren't you? The money and dream situation?'

Jessica floundered in an agonising maelstrom. *She so gets me!* 'Now you bring it up, yes.'

Adriana rubbed Jessica's knee and Jessica's traitorous lips responded with a grin.

'I didn't mean to come across so … evangelical. I know it's hard starting at the bottom.' Jessica arched a sceptical eyebrow and Adriana laughed. 'Okay, I can only imagine how hard it is to struggle with finances.'

As much as it made Jessica feel uncomfortable to talk about her insecurities, she just couldn't stop herself. 'It's not just the money though. I'm useless at everything.'

Adriana nuzzled Jessica's neck. 'I wouldn't go that far. You were amazing last night.'

Jessica giggled as she squirmed in her seat, soon forgetting about her woes. 'So were you.'

'And I would have liked nothing more than to

carry on from where we left off this morning.'

'So why didn't you say something? I would have been happy to oblige.'

Adriana drew back, sighing. 'Because I was pissed off after I got a text—'

'From who?'

Jessica sensed she wasn't going to like what Adriana had to say. The clue was in Adriana's body language. Arms tight across her chest. Eyes narrowed and her back was ramrod straight. Though Jessica thought she was prepared for whatever Adriana threw at her, she couldn't have been more wrong.

'The man …' Adriana said taking her time, '… my parents want me to get engaged to.'

Jessica's stomach tightened. Could her day get any worse? Apparently so, if the grim expression on Adriana's face was anything to go by. 'I thought we were talking hypothetically about marriage. I didn't realise you already had someone lined up?'

Adriana's eyes clouded with uneasiness. 'It's complicated.'

'Okay, so what did ….' Jessica paused, waiting for Adriana to fill in his name.

'Hugo.'

'Want?' Jessica finished.

'To know when I was going home … so we can discuss our future.'

Jessica felt as if someone had punched her in the gut. She had absolutely no idea how to respond. Did she say, 'I'm happy for you both, you'll make a beautiful bride' or did she shake Adriana until she made her see sense?

Jessica swallowed hard, trying to manage a feeble answer. 'That's, um ... nice.'

'This is why I didn't want to tell you.'

Biting her lip until it throbbed, Jessica looked out of the window at the clouds beneath them, suddenly anxious to escape. She thought how nice it would be to be encased in one of the big white fluffy balls floating to everywhere and nowhere.

To be anywhere but here.

Jessica blinked back the tears stinging her eyes before turning back to Adriana. 'Why didn't you want to tell me?'

'Because I knew it would upset you.' Adriana's expression stilled and grew serious. 'Reality is a nasty wake-up call isn't it.'

Jessica shrugged and said with all the bravado she could muster, 'I knew the score before we slept together. That you've already got your life planned out ahead of you.'

'But—'

'There aren't any buts. Finding out you're getting engaged to pugo—'

Adriana's eyes grew openly amused. 'Hugo.'

'Whoever, hasn't come as that much of a surprise,' Jessica said. 'When I get my dosh for finding my nan, I might find a lady myself.'

'You'll forget about me? Will it be that easy?'

Though Jessica felt bereft and desolate, she wasn't

about to let Adriana know that. She shrugged nonchalantly. 'All I know is it's about time I started having a bit of fun.'

'In that case, I'm happy for you.'

'Good and I'm happy for you.' Jessica wondered if it was physically possible for her heart to shatter into tiny segments.

'Good,' Adriana repeated.

'So until we go back home we just enjoy ourselves, yes?' Jessica said like a woman in charge of her own destiny.

'Yes, in fact.' Adriana gestured to the toilet behind their seat with a slow secret smile.

'If you're thinking it's time to join the mile-high club then yes, I agree.' Jessica brightened at the suggestion. Why let the future spoil the present moment? Surely it was best to store as many memories as possible so she could live off them for years to come. And what could be better than having an orgasm thirty-five thousand feet in the air?

'I'll go first. Wait for a couple of minutes before you follow me,' Adriana whispered. She slipped out of her seat, and winked at Jessica before making her way to the lavatory.

Just as Jessica got to her feet, an elderly lady with short permed hair stopped by Adriana's empty seat and bent over to her. 'Do you mind if I sit here a minute dear. Someone's in the toilet.'

I know! She's waiting for me! 'No, of course not.' Jessica slumped down in her seat and patted the empty space beside her.

'Thank you. My names Marge by the way,' she said, slowly squeezing herself onto the seat.

'I'm Jessica.' Seeing all the effort it took Marge to sit down, Jessica knew there was no way in hell she could ask the poor woman to stand up again to let her pass.

'Jessica. Ahh, what a lovely name,' Marge said. 'I would've named my daughter something like that if I'd had one.'

'Did you only have boys then?'

Marge's eyes welled up and Jessica felt like kicking herself. What memories had she forced the poor woman to dredge up. Jessica knew she should say something comforting, but what? Filling awkward silences with useless platitudes wasn't Jessica's forte.

'I wasn't lucky enough to have children,' Marge said turning to look at her. 'My husband, Bill, doesn't like them. Thinks they're noisy buggers.'

'I'm sorry,' Jessica said thankful Marge wasn't about to divulge a tale of death and woe.

'So was I. But I can't complain. I've had a good life. Never wanted for anything.' Marge brushed away a tear that rolled down her cheek. 'But ... oh listen to me being all miserable with myself. We're going to Fiji. At my age, I should be grateful to still be alive.'

'That's the way to think of it,' Jessica said encouragingly.

Just then an elderly man with a head full of thick grey hair came up the aisle, smiling as he neared. 'There you are. Come on, Marge. You didn't have to come all this way. There's a toilet down by us.'

'Is there? Silly me. It's a good thing I remembered to put my teeth in this morning. This is my husband Bill.' Marge held out her hand and let Bill help her out of her seat. 'It was lovely meeting you, Jessica.'

'Nice meeting you both too.' The moment Marge retreated down the aisle with Bill, Jessica rushed to the toilet hoping Adriana was still game for their little rendezvous.

When Jessica tapped on the door, Adriana opened it and all but dragged her inside.

Jessica gave a quick wiggle of her eyebrows then she squeezed and manoeuvred until she could fit into the cramped space.

Without saying a word, Adriana quickly undid the button on Jessica's jeans and slid her hands down her underwear.

Adriana's lips brushed against Jessica's as she spoke. 'What took you so long?'

'Sorry, I got talking to an elderly—' Jessica stopped the moment Adriana's fingers found her clit. Gently, they caressed and massaged her swollen nub, sending a current of pleasure through her. Jessica's hands moved frantically up and down the length of Adriana's back.

'Are you comfortable?'

'Not really,' Jessica said, panting slightly.

'Do you want to stop?' Adriana increased the tempo causing Jessica to writhe against her.

'Are you crazy?' As the last word left her mouth,

Jessica's legs trembled beneath her. She bit her lip to stifle a cry as a surge of energy rushed to her centre and exploded.

Adriana grinned. 'That was quick, I—'

They both cocked their heads when they heard incongruous laughter from outside.

'Mmm, looks like you're going to have to wait for your turn.' Jessica gave Adriana a quick peck on her nose.

'Marge!' Jessica said in surprise as she pulled the door aside with great difficulty. Without thinking, she started fixing her hair. 'Do you still need the loo?'

Marge briefly glanced back at Bill behind her. 'The mile-high club isn't only for youngsters you know.'

'It's not what it looks like.' Heat rushed to Jessica's face and she lowered her gaze to the ground.

'You've embarrassed the poor girl,' Bill said, coming to Jessica's rescue.

'It's good to see a couple still young at heart,' Adriana's voice came from behind as she exited the toilet.

'As long as I've got Marge by my side, I think I will always be a young-un,' Bill said and then kissed Marge softly on her lips.

'We'll let you get on.' Adriana motioned ahead when the seat belt sign came on. 'We'd better get back to our seats.'

'How on earth are they gonna get down to action in that tiddly space?' Jessica asked, clicking her seat belt on.

'Where there's a will there's a way.'

Jessica shook her head to dislodge the image she had conjured up in her mind's eye of poor old Marge and Bill trying to manoeuvre themselves into a comfortable position to get it on. She didn't even want to think of the impact the turbulence was having on their mile-high experience.

Adriana leant in against Jessica, resting her shoulder on her head. 'What's the likelihood of us having another round in the loo?'

'Hmm, let's see … zero.' Jessica gripped the hand rest as the plane dipped and rose in quick succession. It felt as if they were on a roller coaster, and Jessica hated roller coasters with a passion. Fear bubbled over like a volcano and she looked past Adriana to the couple sat opposite, expecting them to be as panic stricken as she was. But the fact that they were acting as if this continuous air bumping was nothing out of the ordinary, scared her even more. They were obviously panicking as much as she was but were much better at hiding it.

Adriana tugged at Jessica's hand until she finally loosened her grip. 'Try and relax, the turbulence won't last for long. Look.'

Steeling herself, Jessica's gaze followed Adriana's finger to the screen in front of them which showed the remaining distance and time. Reassured by the green patches of land, Jessica reasoned that even if the plane did crash, it wouldn't be in open waters. She would welcome any fate but that one.

By the time the plane landed in Fiji, Jessica had drunk four gin and tonics and could still feel the fear. She couldn't help but wonder where pilots got the courage to fly planes. If she were at the controls, she'd be screaming at the slightest noise, let alone anything else.

As they entered the terminal, Jessica switched on her phone to check if her grandmother had called but there were no messages. Passing through passport control, the passengers were greeted by a group of men and women in grass skirts performing a traditional dance. The warm welcome literally brought tears to Jessica's eyes. Everything felt right in the world, even with the knowledge that there was a man waiting back in the UK hoping to make Adriana his wife.

'Oh my God, those dancers were amazing,' Jessica said once they were settled in the back of a taxi.

Adriana nodded in agreement as she wound down her window. Instead of the sweltering heat and humidity of Australia, the air felt cool and fresh.

'Just imagine, if it wasn't for your nan and her letter, I would never have experienced all of this in a million years,' Jessica said, refraining from adding, *and I wouldn't have met you.*

'Don't be so pessimistic. You don't know how your life's going to turn out.'

Jessica's short bark of laughter lacked humour. 'That's where you're wrong. I know exactly what's going to happen. And from where I'm sitting, it's not looking that good.'

'Do you know what your problem is?'

'Go on, shock me.'

Adriana reached over and took her hand, holding it snugly in her own. 'You don't have any self-belief. You want to play life's victim instead of taking responsibility for yourself. Do you think people who have made a success of their life sat around waiting, like the world owed them a favour? Thinking that someone was going to come along and put their dream in their hands for them? It's your life, Jessica, and if you want it to be a successful one, only you can make that happen.'

'Yes but doing what?' Jessica was uncomfortable with the fact that Adriana had spoken the truth and it made her somewhat defensive. 'It's all very well with the "Run after your dream" speech, but what if you truly don't have one?'

'Then go and see a life coach. Believe it or not, if you find the right one they can work wonders in your life.'

Though Jessica's mind was congested with doubt and fear, she liked the sound of that idea. Her very own life coach to help her map out her future. To help her find the dream that she knew had to exist somewhere within. If Jessica found her nan she would have the money to hire one, so there'd be no excuses for not achieving anything.

'You know; a life coach sounds cool. I think that's the way to go.'

Adriana squeezed her hand but didn't let go of it until the taxi pulled up outside a small resort set over two levels, overlooking a rainforest. A thin short man, wearing a flower garland opened the cab door and offered them a drink from the tray he held in his hands.

This was the kind of lifestyle Jessica could get used to, she thought, taking one. She had never seen so many happy looking people in her life. *Maybe it's because they live in a sunny climate.* That actually made sense when she thought about it. The UK's skies were normally blanketed with grey miserable clouds, so it was hardly surprising that the population mirrored them.

Drink in hand, they followed, who she now knew to be Vishal, into the reception area where he gestured for them to sign in at the reception desk. The resort wasn't as fancy as the hotel in Sydney, but the panoramic view of endless turquoise ocean was so spectacular that it would have been impossible to decide which one was the nicer of the two.

'Hi, we'd like to check in please, and also we phoned ahead and left a message for Edwina Wilson who is staying here but we haven't heard back from her,' Adriana said when they approached the male receptionist.

'No problem, madam. I will check for you now.'

'Okay, thank you,' Adriana replied.

After several minutes tapping on his computer, the receptionist glanced up at them both, a confused expression on his face. 'I'm afraid I cannot find any record of your message, but don't worry I will ring through to her room for you now. What's your name please?'

'It's Jessica Wilson, I'm her granddaughter.'

The receptionist picked up the phone on the reception desk and tapped in a number. 'I'm afraid there is no answer,' he said after replacing the receiver a minute later. 'She may have gone on a day trip, we have several on today. I will place a note on her account to let her know what room you are in when she returns.'

'Okay, thank you for your help,' Jessica said.

After checking in, they made their way to their room on the first floor. Stepping inside the air-conditioned space, Jessica looked around. The room was nothing to write home about. It was as basic as basic could be—twin beds, a cabinet and a small TV and balcony that overlooked the entrance below. But it was their little hideaway and that's all that mattered.

'So ....' Jessica embraced Adriana and moved against her in a suggestive body caress. 'While we're waiting, do you want to re-enact the mile-high club experience in the bathroom?'

Adriana pressed against her. 'Do you think it will be the same? I mean there's no chance of us getting caught.'

'I could always leave our hotel room door open.' Jessica lowered her mouth to Adriana's neck, planting little kisses on her faintly fragranced skin. 'A really hot cleaner might come in and see us.'

As Adriana's hands slid underneath Jessica's top and up her back, Jessica felt a sensation of intense desolation sweep over her at the thought that one day, in the not too distant future, Adriana's hands would burn a path down Hugo's back. Would she be having sex marathons with him? Call out his name in the throes of passion? Just thinking it made her sick to the stomach. Jessica broke free suddenly, her mind in a flurry.

'What's wrong?' Adriana asked, eyeing her with concern.

'Nothing.' She walked over to her case and unzipped it, pretending to look for something, hoping that Adriana wouldn't probe any further. How stupid had she been? Thinking that she could indulge in a brief affair had opened the floodgates on a tsunami of feelings that she didn't realise she had.

Jessica wasn't the kind of cool, laid back twenty-something who went with the flow. In hindsight, if she hadn't allowed her hormones to be in charge, things would never have gone this far.

But now her heart was going to have to pay the price for her carelessness. She'd enclosed herself in a bubble in her desire to break free, to become someone else, even for a few days, and that bubble had now burst. Adriana had been right—reality was a nasty wake up call.

'So are we going to play in the bathroom?' The intention was clear in Adriana's voice and a few minutes ago Jessica was totally up for it. But now, realising that no matter how much she wanted to believe Adriana could have feelings for her that extended beyond sex, Jessica knew she had just been deluding herself.

'Actually, I was thinking I'd have a look round the

hotel and see if I can find my nan. She might not be on a trip.' Jessica looked up at Adriana, willing herself to be strong and not falter. 'You stay here and relax, I'll let you know if I find her.'

'If that's what you want.'

'It is.' Jessica pushed herself to her feet. The best thing she could do right now was give them both some breathing space.'

'OK. See you in a while.'

'Cool.' Jessica stumbled over her case as she hurried from the room. Once outside, she leant against a wall in the stairwell and inhaled deeply, then exhaled. Her heart pounded against her ribcage, as if it was grieving for the love that it knew would be denied.

Jessica walked around the small hotel, she checked by the pool and in the restaurant but saw no sign of her nan. The receptionist had kindly given Jessica her nan's room number so she went there next and knocked on the door. When no one answered, Jessica placed her ear up against the door. *Nothing.*

Not wanting to go back to their room just yet, Jessica headed to the bar where she consumed two very tall cocktails in rapid succession. In between drinks, she told the barman about their search for her nan. And in response, Ratu had told her about a horse riding tour that was the number one attraction for tourists young and old. He suggested she go and see Timoci, the owner, as he would be able to help them. It was a long shot, but it beat sitting around the hotel all day waiting for her to turn up.

When Jessica returned to their room and ran the idea by Adriana, she was pleasantly surprised when Adriana agreed with Ratu's suggestion.

Soon they were driving in the direction of the stables. Everything in Fiji was green and the sky was a clear blue. The ocean ran alongside the road they travelled and if Jessica hadn't seen it with her own eyes, she would never have believed the sea could be so impossibly transparent.

Jessica was soon feeling the effect of the cocktails she had drunk at the hotel and the drinks on the plane. Rather than feeling queasy, a sense of melancholy overwhelmed her. Not only about her own sad life, but that of her nan's who had never found love again after her granddad had died. Also about Adriana who was going to be pressured into an arranged marriage to a man she didn't love. And guilt about her own parents who, through no fault of their own, had never been on a plane before. That they had lived their forty years in London and hadn't even seen a glimpse of the world.

Adriana gave her a cold bottle of water from her bag and Jessica obediently drank it.

The driver soon stopped at a local viewpoint and Jessica and Adriana got out on either side of the taxi. Jessica used her hand to shield her eyes from the sun as she took in the turquoise coastline. It only took one look at her surroundings to realise why her nan would love Fiji.

Chapter Fifteen

'Can you believe how difficult it is to find her?' Jessica asked Adriana once they were back in the taxi and heading towards their destination.

'I know, it's insane.' Adriana pinched the bridge of her nose to head off the stress headache she could feel building.

'It's unbelievable to think I'm sixty years younger than my nan and even I haven't got the energy to keep going at her pace.' Jessica's voice was flat.

'It's not too late to develop a zest for life.'

'So you keep saying,' Jessica said as she hunched further into the corner of the seat.

Jessica's withdrawal signalled that Adriana wasn't being paranoid. That something really was amiss. She had noticed Jessica's sudden change of behaviour back at the hotel. Adriana wasn't that naïve not to realise what the cause of it was.

Because, despite Jessica's attempt to come across as being blasé about Hugo, Adriana knew finding out about him had cut Jessica to the bone. And she totally got why. She really did. After all, they had slept together and had the best sex she'd ever thought possible.

As well as this, they were completely compatible. In every possible way. A perfect match.

Well it would have been in another world. *Another time*.

It depressed Adriana to think about the future, but

this time tomorrow they could be making their way home, and home meant family and obligations.

Home meant a life that didn't include Jessica.

'Just to let you know, I have a fear of horses,' Jessica said, once the taxi had dropped them by a small stick shack that had 'Reception' spray painted along the bottom.

'Have you ridden before then?' Adriana asked, looking around her immediate surroundings in the hope of seeing a member of staff.

With a shuddering breath, Jessica shook her head. 'No way, their eyes are too dodgy. They stare too much for my liking.'

'You think?' Adriana stifled a giggle. Jessica said the most outlandish things sometimes. It was obvious by her response to most things they encountered that she had led a sheltered life and hadn't been exposed to the many things Adriana took for granted. But to think a horse had 'dodgy' eyes because they stared at you, that was a first, even for her.

A man with short grey air appeared on a horse from behind. His face was deeply lined and a wide smile revealed crooked teeth as he approached them.

'Welcome ladies, Timoci at your service.' Timoci climbed down from the horse with ease. 'You've come to the best place for a tour of the beautiful forest?'

'Actually.' Jessica stepped forward. 'We'd like to know if you recognise this woman. If maybe she's on one of your tours today?'

Jessica held out the picture of Edwina, and

Timoci's face fell as he shook his head. 'Sorry.'

'Don't worry. Not all is lost,' Adriana said eyeing Timoci's horse with relish. It had been a while since she'd been riding and as Jessica had never experienced it before, Adriana thought it would be a crime to pass up an opportunity to teach Jessica she had nothing to fear from horses.

'What are you doing?' Jessica asked when Adriana took money out of her bag and handed it to Timoci.

'Seeing as we're here, we might as well have some fun,' Adriana said.

'I can see you're nervous,' Timoci said to Jessica. 'But don't worry, Black Beauty is a good horse. I just need to give her a drink.'

When Timoci took Black Beauty by the reins and led her away, Jessica looked at Adriana in horror. 'I don't want to ride Black Beauty. In fact, I don't want to ride any horse—'

'Oh, come on, where's your sense of adventure? Don't you want to experience new things?' Adriana said in a cajoling manner.

'No,' Jessica replied bluntly.

'Well, then do it for me then. I really want to see the sights—'

'No one's stopping you. I'm more than happy to wait in the car.'

Adriana shrugged and handed her bag to Jessica as Timoci steered Black Beauty towards them. 'Suit yourself. Stay in your comfort zone, see if I care.'

'My comfort zone? I'll show you!' Jessica said. She

strode towards Timoci and within seconds she was mounted on Black Beauty's back. 'What are you waiting for? You coming?'

'You bet.' Adriana smiled as Timoci gave her a helping hand.

'Please tell me you've ridden a horse before.' Jessica tightened her arms around Adriana's waist as she gave Black Beauty a gentle tap of her heels.

'Of course I have,' Adriana said. 'I used to ride in competitions all the time.'

'You don't know how happy I am to hear that.'

Adriana stroked Black Beauty's head. 'You're a beautiful girl, aren't you?'

They followed the scenic route Timoci had suggested. The dirt path wound downwards amongst lush foliage, and an iguana scurried past causing Jessica to jump.

Adriana laughed. 'Don't worry, it won't hurt you.'

'What makes you think I was worried?' Jessica replied, her voice a little shaky.

Adriana smiled at Jessica's false bravado.

Soon they came to a fork in the road with a sign for the lagoon Timoci had insisted they see. The clear water looked breathtakingly beautiful as they neared. Adriana tilted her head, convinced she could hear water running.

'Can you hear that?'

'The only things I can hear are the horse's hooves and the pounding of my heart between my ears. But you're not talking about either of those, are you?'

'No.' Adriana suddenly gasped. 'Look.'

'What!' Jessica jerked backwards nearly falling off the horse and Adriana instinctively reached back for her. 'Have you seen a snake?'

'Hey, relax you're going to spook the horse,' Adriana said. 'It's just a waterfall.'

'Oh.' The relief in Jessica's voice was evident. 'Sorry. I hate snakes.'

Adriana briefly looked over her shoulder at Jessica. 'Have you even seen a snake in real life?'

'Well no, not exactly,' Jessica admitted. 'But that doesn't make them any less dangerous.'

Adriana pulled back on the reins causing Black Beauty to come to a halt. 'Come on, let's go and take a closer look.'

'Are you sure there aren't any—'

'I promise you. There aren't any snakes.' Adriana dismounted and held out her hand to help Jessica down. Tying the reins to a tree stump near the edge of the lagoon, Adriana and Jessica walked in the direction of the waterfall. Seeing the magnificence of nature's creation up close, took Adriana's breath away.

'Hey, what are you doing?' Jessica asked, a crease of worry lined her forehead when Adriana kicked off her sandals, slipped out of her shirt, then her jeans and underwear.

'Going for a swim.'

'Are you crazy?' Jessica said frantically looking around. 'What if—'

'What if what? A shark eats me? Or a rock falls on

my head?'

One corner of Jessica's mouth pulled into a slight smile. 'Well, yeah, you never know.'

Adriana cupped Jessica's face with the palms of her hands. 'You've got to start living, Jess, and stop worrying about what if. Your life will pass you by and you will have done nothing. Don't let fear stop you from living.'

Adriana tilted Jessica's chin, kissed her lightly on the mouth then walked to the edge of the lagoon and lowered herself in.

'Wait!'

Adriana paused and turned back to see Jessica hastily removing her clothes as she called out. 'I'm coming too.'

Jessica dumped her clothes in a pile, took Adriana's outstretched hand and joined her in the lukewarm water. Side by side they swam over to the waterfall, stopping directly beneath it.

'Oh my God! I'm under a waterfall! I'm under a waterfall!' Jessica shouted to make her voice audible over the noise of the cascading water.

'I wish I had a camera to capture this moment.' Jessica wrapped her arms around Adriana's neck.

'You don't need a camera. It's all in your memory,' Adriana said loud enough to be heard.

Adriana pulled Jessica closer to her, embracing her tightly and kissing her firmly on her lips. Jessica immediately responded by parting her lips, allowing Adriana's tongue to explore the warmth of her mouth.

At that moment, Adriana felt a rush of emotion she had never experienced before. All her worries, fears and concerns about the future evaporated as the water rained down upon them. Adriana moved her hands across Jessica's breasts gently caressing them as their kiss deepened and their souls entwined.

Jessica drew back suddenly, her gaze sparkling with happiness. 'I—'

The noise from the water crashing on the rocks drowned out the sound of Jessica's voice. Adriana knew what Jessica had said and it brought her back to reality with a thud. *What was I thinking?* This was not how this trip was meant to turn out. Once the L word was mentioned they were treading in uncharted waters.

Finally coming to her senses, Adriana moved backwards.

'We should get going,' she said, swimming away without checking to see if Jessica was following.

'I'm sorry,' Jessica said softly when they were both dressed and back on Black Beauty.

Adriana kept her gaze in front of her and her tone even. 'You've got nothing to apologise for.'

'I—'

'Look, I said you haven't,' Adriana snapped. 'So let's leave it at that.'

'Okay. Whatever you say,' Jessica said, her voice unsure. 'So what shall we do now?'

'I don't think your nan is here. Why wouldn't she have contacted you by now? I don't think the hotel know what they are talking about.'

'But they said she's here and gave me the room number. Why would they make it up?'

'I don't know, they just seem incompetent. I'm starting to think we're wasting our time and we should head home. I have a life I need to get back to.' Adriana made the decision without even giving it much thought.

'To Hugo?'

Adriana heard the sadness in Jessica's voice, the slight tremor in her body against Adriana's back. But there was nothing that she could do or say to fix this. It was what it was. As soon as they got back to the hotel, Adriana knew what she had to do. The first thing would be to call her father and ask him to book their tickets back to the UK on the next flight out.

'To everything. I have work, friends, family.' Adriana let out a frustrated breath as she steered Black Beauty back towards the stables. 'I don't exist in my own little cocoon.'

'Like me?' Jessica said so sadly a flash of wild grief ripped through Adriana.

'I never said that.'

Jessica's voice broke miserably. 'You didn't have to.'

Adriana sensed Jessica was seeking some sort of resolution to the situation they both found themselves in. But Adriana couldn't go there. She didn't want to open herself up to this emotional drama. She would have enough of that from her parents when she returned home.

'Let's just drop this, shall we? We both know

where we stand so there's really nothing more to say.'

The short journey back to the stable was made in an awkward silence. The joy from sightseeing now gone. All Adriana could think about was how she was going to get through the next couple of days without breaking down and giving in to temptation.

When they returned to the taxi, Adriana opted to sit in the front under the pretence that she suffered from car sickness when seated in the back. The driver accepted her excuse without a bat of an eyelid, but Jessica looked at her downtrodden.

Maybe it was for the best Jessica thought of Adriana as an uncaring bitch without a heart. That way it would be easier for Jessica to move on rather than spend her time romancing a fantasy that had no way of becoming a reality.

And as for Adriana? Jessica aside, the first thing she needed to do was sort out her grandmother's apartment. Seeing as she would be going home without her inheritance sorted, she would have to call in a favour from one of her friends and ask them to put an offer in on the property for her.

Edwina would hopefully return home within three months so Adriana's inheritance could be released. And if Edwina didn't return in time for the completion date, Adriana would use her own apartment as collateral to pay for it.

Glancing at Jessica in the side mirror, Adriana's heart ached at the thought of saying goodbye to her, but staying with Jessica any longer than absolutely necessary was a risk Adriana wasn't willing to take.

Chapter Sixteen

Jessica silently berated herself for spoiling what should have been the most romantic moment of her life on the drive back to the resort. Making love with Adriana under a waterfall. It was like a scene from a movie. And she just had to put a spanner in the works because she couldn't hold back. Couldn't keep her mouth shut and her thoughts in her head.

When they reached the reception, Jessica enquired again about her grandmother's whereabouts.

'I'm afraid Mrs Wilson checked out early this morning,' the female receptionist said.

'But the person earlier told me she was here! And I left messages with you,' Jessica exclaimed.

'I'm very sorry, there appears to have been a miscommunication.'

'Just leave it, Jessica, I told you she wasn't here,' Adriana said.

When they got back to their room, Adriana said she had started her period and was going to have a long soak in the bath to combat her period pain. Yes, she might well have been telling the truth, and Jessica might well have believed her had it not been for the fact Adriana had barely spoken to her since they left the lagoon.

When Adriana still hadn't made an appearance two hours later, Jessica knew their 'fling' had come to an abrupt end. Jessica had unwittingly overstepped the mark and she only had herself to blame. What had she been thinking? Blurting out that she loved Adriana. What kind of fool would do that? *Someone hopelessly in love, that's who.*

There was no point in her trying to deny her feelings any longer. Even her hand couldn't control the way it felt as it scribbled on the hotel's notepad:

Jessica loves Adriana Jessica 4 Adriana.

Jessica hadn't meant to spook Adriana with her confession, only express how much she cared about her. And she had hoped, no, prayed that by some miracle Adriana felt the same way about her. That the arrangement she had with Hugo was something their true love would overcome. *Obviously not!*

Dropping the pen on the table, Jessica stared ahead watching the birds duck and dive in the darkening sky. What could she possibly offer Adriana that 'Mr Rich Balls' couldn't offer ten times over. Money, security, kids … all the things Adriana had mentioned were important. *But I could give her my heart. Surely that's worth all the money in the world.* To someone out there it might be, but not to Adriana where it was all about obligations and family.

Jessica could just picture Adriana's parents sitting at an oval antique dining table polishing the family silver. *No scratch that, they'd be watching the hired help polish the family silver.* And they'd be drinking out of china teacups saying what a wonderful match Hugo was for Adriana. How handsome. How talented. How rich. *How sickening!*

Jessica felt her nails digging into the flesh of her hand when she thought about them together. Scoffing into their cups, sounding like a pair of horses when they spoke about the benefits such a match would bring to the family name. They obviously didn't give a damn about Adriana's happiness. How could they if they wanted to marry their only daughter off to a man she didn't love? Couldn't love. Jessica didn't know which was worse, the fact that Adriana was no doubt looked upon like a prized possession. Something so fragile that only a 'man' could take care of her needs. Or that in 2017 the unspoken rule of marrying for the sake of financial and social status still existed. *Okay, they're both as bad as each other,* she decided.

Suddenly Jessica heard Adriana's voice calling her and she looked behind her. Adriana was stood by the bed, mobile phone in hand and an unreadable expression on her face.

Fearing the worst, Jessica jumped to her feet.

'Everything all right?' Jessica asked, knowing full well it wasn't. She could tell by the way Adriana was avoiding her eyes.

'I just spoke to my father. He's in the process of booking our flights. I'm sure you're just as eager to get home and back to your life as I am.'

'Yeah, can't wait. It's a good thing we didn't unpack.' Jessica gestured to their suitcases still by the door.

'Suppose. Do you need to use the bathroom?'

'No. Are you getting back in the bath?' *Surely not.*

Not on our last night together.

Adriana nodded. 'It's the only way to help with the pain.'

Jessica shook her head doubtfully. 'In that case, I think I'll have an early night.'

Adriana opened her mouth to speak but seemed to quickly change her mind. Her gaze dropped to the floor as she walked back to the bathroom and closed the door gently behind her.

Humiliation burnt Jessica's cheeks making them feel as though they could actually spark into flames. *I need to get this into perspective*, she told herself as she slid into bed *alone*. Jessica couldn't let herself have a meltdown. No promises had been made. No utterings of a happily ever after. Just a plain and simple—enjoy it while you can. And Jessica had. There was no denying that, but it still didn't mean Jessica hadn't hoped it wouldn't morph into something else. Something more permanent.

What was needed was a plan of action, so when they returned home, she didn't sit around sulking, pining for Adriana. It was going to be tough but if there was one thing that Jessica was, it was tough and *broke*, she quickly reminded herself. The hundred grand would no longer be on the horizon because, through no fault of her own, she hadn't managed to find her nan.

Jessica squeezed her eyes shut, not wanting to think about her employment status just yet. But as always, what she resisted persisted. She knew she was going to have to make a decision about the Sleazy Slum before the plane touched down in the UK.

If Jessica had any sense, she would march into the bathroom and convince Adriana to continue with their quest. To promise her that she would leave her emotions at the door. The only thing that stopped her was the realisation that it was too late to turn back the clock.

***

It was so surreal. One day Jessica was sitting in a hotel room in Fiji and the next she was on her way back to London. In her naivety, Jessica had thought that Adriana's resolve would somehow melt as she came to the realisation that they would soon be parting ways. But as always, the stories Jessica made up in her mind weren't even close to reality. They had left early in the morning to make a connection to the flight home. Only this time it wasn't in economy. It was business class. Which was cool, but it also meant there was a barrier between them. Which Jessica realised had been a deliberate ploy on Adriana's behalf. It afforded her the ability to remain hidden for most of the journey home. The only time she lowered the slider was when meals were served or she needed to use the loo. For the life of her Jessica couldn't understand what she had done that it warranted the stony silence. An impenetrable invisible wall. And when they finally arrived in London, Adriana's attitude didn't change.

'Well, I'm sorry things didn't work out with finding your grandmother,' Adriana said as they made their way out of the terminal.

'Me too,' Jessica replied coolly. Maybe when Adriana dropped her home, she could invite her upstairs for a coffee. Anything to buy some more time with her. But alas, it seemed that wasn't meant to be.

'Would you mind getting a taxi home,' Adriana said when they stopped outside on the pavement. 'I need to drop by my parents' house, and I'm too tired to drive all the way to yours.'

Drop by your parents' house to discuss things about Hugo? Why doesn't she just come out and say it? It wasn't as if Adriana could hurt her any more than she already had. 'Don't worry about it. I'll get the tube.'

'No, get a taxi, I'll pay—'

'I don't want your money, Adriana,' Jessica said abruptly. When she saw a flicker of pain cloud Adriana's eyes she softened her voice. 'What I mean is, you've paid for enough—'

'I don't mind.'

'No really, it's all right. It will be quicker by tube anyway. Less traffic.'

'If you're sure?'

'I'm positive,' Jessica said.

'So this is it then.' Adriana clasped her hands in front of her.

'Yeah,' Jessica said sadly. The thought of never seeing Adriana again tore at her insides. 'This is it. I had a really good time.'

'Me too.'

Jessica rigidly held her tears in check. 'Did you?

Really?'

'Yes.' There was a faint tremor in Adriana's voice, as though some emotion had touched her.

For a moment, when Adriana took a step towards her, Jessica thought she was going to embrace her, tell her that she'd made a terrible mistake returning home so soon. That of course this wasn't the end. It was merely the beginning. Unfortunately, that idea was soon shot down in flames as Adriana simply pulled a hair off Jessica's jacket.

'You'd better get off then,' Jessica said.

'Suppose I had. Take care of yourself, Jess.' Adriana smiled. 'And try and live out of the box a little.'

'And you try and live by your own rules,' Jessica countered.

'Seems we've both got things in our lives we need to sort out.'

And with that Adriana slipped on her glasses, grabbed the handle to her cases and walked away.

Jessica remained rooted to the spot long after Adriana had disappeared from view. All she had to take away with her was a head full of memories and a broken heart that she knew could never be fixed.

Hours later as she lay on her sofa, Adriana's last act had flummoxed her. That she couldn't bear to be in Jessica's company long enough to drop her home, made her think there was more to her behaviour than simply being annoyed with her because Jessica dared to try and tell her how she felt.

'You know some people just can't handle emotions.'

Ariel looked up at Jessica from where she sat on the floor. 'That's why those types of women only have brief encounters.'

'Types?'

Ariel met Jessica's gaze head on. 'You know, rich totties.'

Jessica shot Ariel a look of disapproval for using such a derogatory word. Adriana was not a 'rich totty' and despite how upset she was, Jessica would not have anyone be disrespectful about Adriana.

'I'm still confused by her giving me the cold shoulder for two days before we got home. I mean, that's not normal, is it?'

'Not being horrible, but she might have thought if you felt that strongly about her you might start stalking her.'

'Me, stalk Adriana? Like I'd have the energy to do that,' Jessica said, astonished that anyone could think such a thing about her.

'Really?' Ariel said with a wry smile. 'So why, since you've been back, have you done nothing but check Adriana's Facebook page?'

'That's not stalking.' Jessica paused, trying to find a more accurate way of describing her actions. One that didn't paint her in such a bad light. 'Me checking out her Facebook is called being nosy.'

Ariel eyed Jessica as if she was being delusional. 'Whatever you say.'

'It's true. How many people do you know who don't stalk, I mean look at their ex's social media?'

'I'm sorry to tell you this, Jess, but she's not your ex. You slept with her what—'

'Around five times, on the same night,' Jessica said, feeling her stomach clench just thinking about it.

'That doesn't count if it happened on one night.'

'Okay, so what about on the plane?'

'If you're that desperate, I'll give you that one as well. So that's twice you did the deed.'

'And don't forget we nearly did it under the waterfall,' Jessica hastily added.

Ariel rolled her eyes. 'You're really scraping the barrel now.'

'Okay,' Jessica conceded. 'So what's your point?'

'My point.' Ariel pushed herself up onto the sofa, forcing Jessica to move into a sitting position. 'Is that you're making more out of this than is real. You're not that naïve to realise that your worlds are miles apart.'

'Why, because I don't speak with a posh accent and I'm not loaded?'

Ariel grinned. 'And you don't have a cock.'

'She isn't straight, Ariel.'

Ariel turned serious. 'That's what she told you. Who knows what she is. If I'm honest people like her—'

'Like her?' Jessica said defensively. 'Why do you keep talking about her as if she's from another planet. What the hell does "people like her" actually mean? That because she's rich, she's half human or something?'

Ariel extended her hand and took hold of Jessica's. 'No of course not. I mean in the sense that how she views the world is different to ours. They operate on a completely different level. We have to fight to survive every single day, but my guess is Adriana has never had to wonder if she was going to have enough money to pay her rent at the end of the month. Or if she'll have enough food in the fridge.'

'But that's not her fault.' Jessica's eyes welled with tears. The world was so unjust.

'I didn't say it was. I'm just saying in the nicest possible way.' Ariel's voice softened. 'Adriana's out of your league. She knows it and her behaviour suggests she's trying to let you know as well.'

'That's crap.' Jessica snatched her hand away. 'Adriana isn't that shallow and if you had spent time with her like I did, you'd know that too.'

'I didn't mean to upset you.'

Jessica stood, feeling incredibly dizzy as she did. 'I feel like shit; I'm going to sleep. I think I've got jetlag.'

'Do you want me to go home?'

'Nah.' Jessica stifled a yawn. 'You can stay as long as you like.'

'Brilliant. The thought of going back to my parents fills me with dread,' Ariel said, pulling a face. 'Don't get me wrong, they're great, but there's a good reason birds leave the nest.'

As Jessica sat on the edge of her bed she suddenly said, 'Ariel, do you want to share a flat?'

Ariel frowned as she looked around the room. 'Here? I love ya, babe, but I think we'd be at each other's throats within a day.'

'Not here. A two-bed place?'

Ariel beamed. 'Really? If you're serious—yes, yes and yes!'

'Cool, use my laptop to look on Rightmove. I'll check out what you've found when I wake up.'

'I'm on it,' Ariel said, flipping Jessica's laptop lid open.

Although tiredness was the main reason for Jessica going to bed, it wasn't the only one. In her heart of hearts, she knew Ariel's assessment of the situation was the right one. Jessica was only kidding herself if she thought any different. But as much as she wanted to hold on to the dream that there was a chance for them, she knew she was going to have to let it go. And sooner rather than later.

Jessica rested her head on the pillow with a new resolve. She was no longer going to be a shrinking violet. If there was one thing she had learnt from her short jaunt with Adriana, it was that there was a whole new world out there for her to explore. As well as sexual relationships. Until now, Jessica hadn't realised how much she missed the feel of a naked woman. *Adriana.* Her touch, smell, sound ….

Wake up! Wake up! Wake up! A voice screeched in Jessica's head. Heart pounding against her chest, Jessica sprang into a sitting position. Something didn't feel right. In fact, she couldn't feel at all. Her arm! In a daze, she picked it up with her right hand and held it in the air. It hung like a dead weight. *I hate it when that happens.* With as much energy as she could muster, she shook it in an attempt to wake it up and her nerve endings soon began to prickle from her fingertips upwards.

The living room was pitch black which told her she must have been asleep for hours. Her mouth was as dry as a bone and she slipped out of bed and went in search of water.

Taking a bottle of water from the fridge, Jessica drank from it as she glanced over at Ariel curled up on the sofa fast asleep, the TV remote control still in her hand.

Spotting her mobile phone on the coffee table, Jessica picked it up then leant over and took the control from Ariel's hand. She absent-mindedly glanced down at her phone and realised the blue light was flashing, indicating a message. She stared down at it galvanised. It was a text message from Adriana, sent at 10pm. With a start, Jessica saw it was five in the morning. She had slept for over twelve hours. No wonder she had woken with a dead arm.

Jessica knew she was stalling from reading the message as she dreaded to see what Adriana had to tell her. Would it be news about her engagement to Hugo and how happy she was? No, Adriana wouldn't be that cruel. Perhaps she'd opened the letter to Jessica's nan and wanted to tell her what was inside. Whatever it was, Jessica could no longer put it off. Good news or bad news, she had to know.

Tapping on the message, she blinked a few times to make sure she wasn't hallucinating. She wasn't. It was short and to the point.

I need to see you.

Chapter Seventeen

Adriana swiped her perspiring forehead with the back of her hand. This was exactly what she needed. Something that made her heart race, her adrenaline pump and most importantly take her mind off the thing called her life. She pressed the button on the treadmill taking it up to 7mph and her feet pounded the floor. Another ten minutes and she was done. She had been at the gym since 6am. One of the many benefits of having a gym in her apartment building was that she could go whenever she wanted. Which was great for an early riser like herself.

Although the flight back from Australia had taken its toll on her sleep cycle, Adriana wasn't the type to give in to tiredness. She did what she wanted to do, not what her body insisted on doing.

Besides, if Adriana hadn't been in the gym keeping her mind occupied, she would have driven herself crazy with thoughts about Jessica and why she hadn't responded to the message she had sent her the previous night. Not that she blamed her for ignoring it. Adriana knew she'd behaved appallingly and it was so out of character that she barely recognised herself. But she had been so unprepared for that moment under the waterfall; Jessica had totally blindsided her. Not that she blamed Jessica, who was only owning up to her feelings. But by doing so, she had forced her to face up to the truth about how she felt about Jessica. Which Adriana did not need right now.

As she walked at a slower pace, the door to the gym opened and Imogen strode in, not looking the slightest bit pleased at being woken at such an early hour in the morning.

'I love you, Addy, but I swear to God, if this isn't important, I'm going to kill you.'

Adriana stepped off the treadmill, took a swig of water and patted her face with her towel. 'It is. First, thanks for coming.'

'Never mind thanking me, just explain what you couldn't tell me over the phone then I'm going back to bed.'

'Let's go up to my apartment,' Adriana said. 'I'll make you a latte.'

For the first time, a smile broke out on Imogen's face. 'Now you're talking.'

'I need your help,' Adriana said, as they walked along the corridor to the lift.

'I gathered as much.'

They stepped into the lift and Adriana pressed the button for the penthouse. 'My aunt wants to sell my grandmother's apartment.'

Imogen scowled. 'What a bitch. I never liked her. There's something very shifty about her.'

'I know. But my mum can't stop her, which means unless I buy it, all of the memories that place holds will be gone forever.'

Adriana turned to look at Imogen whose eyes mirrored her own sadness. Beatrice had been like a surrogate grandmother to her.

'So how can I help?' Imogen said. 'I'll do anything.'

'I need you to put an offer in for her apartment.'

'Okay,' was all she said, as if Adriana had just asked her to take a jog in the park with her.

'Is that it?' Adriana said. 'Okay?'

'Did you expect me to say no?' Imogen said as they stepped out of the lift and walked the short distance to Adriana's apartment. 'But this isn't why you really called me over, is it?'

Adriana opened her front door and made her way to her bedroom, calling over her shoulder. 'You know me too well. I'm just going to shower and change. There's caviar in the fridge.'

Ten minutes later Adriana re-emerged, dressed in jeans and a waistcoat. Imogen was sat at the island in the centre of the kitchen spooning caviar onto a blini.

'Is this about Hugo?' Imogen eyed Adriana as she crossed over to the coffee machine and inserted a pod.

'Yes and no.' Adriana removed a bottle of milk from the fridge and poured half of it into a milk warmer and switched it on.

'That sounds ambiguous.' Imogen popped the blini into her mouth.

'I've fallen for someone. Hard.' Adriana could not believe she was actually saying this out loud. But the thoughts that had been going around and around in her head had been driving her crazy. Her heart yearned for Jessica's love. While her body ached for her touch.

Imogen's eyes widened. 'What! I mean who?

Rather how? You've only been. Oh my goodness, no.' Imogen burst out laughing, covering her mouth with her hand. 'Not the little vixen you went globetrotting with?'

'The one and only,' Adriana said, taking two latte glasses out of the cupboard.

'Now I know you're being ridiculous and you've spoilt a completely wonderful sleep I was enjoying.'

'I'm not joking, Imogen.' This was the last thing Adriana had wanted or expected. Why would any sane person want to be in a state of anxiety because someone hadn't returned their message? Or walk around feeling as if a part of themselves was missing? This 'love' thing that people sought out above all other things was crazy. Absolutely, insanely … amazing! In truth, Adriana had never felt this alive before. Had never lived with such anticipation.

'Well of course you are,' Imogen said. 'You can't fall for a woman. Not seriously anyway. There's too much at stake.'

'Don't you think I know that.' Adriana filled the glasses with coffee and handed one to Imogen. 'But I can't help how I feel.'

'Then you're going to have to give yourself a bloody good talking to. I mean seriously, Addy, not even a woman of any means. A poor person—'

'Don't be so snobbish,' Adriana snapped. 'I thought you of all people would understand.'

'I do and that's why I'm advising you to steer clear.' Imogen blew on her coffee before taking a sip.

'It'll all end in tears if you don't.'

'Are you telling me, hand on heart, you don't think about that woman you had an affair with?' Adriana said, knowing full well if Imogen said no, calling her over had been a complete and utter waste of time. If she couldn't be truthful with her, there was no way Imogen could ever give her sound advice. To her relief, Imogen was anything but reluctant to tell the truth.

'Of course I think about her, but that doesn't mean I regret letting her go. I have obligations and so do you.'

'But why?' Adriana said, knowing full well she sounded like a spoilt brat who wanted everything her own way. 'Why should I have to forsake my own happiness for a sodding family name.'

'Because it's the done thing and has been for generations. How do you think we survive? We have to follow rules. And one of them is that we stick to our own kind.'

'Fuck the rules,' Adriana said, slamming her cup on the counter, causing the liquid to spill. 'I don't care.'

'You don't care?' Imogen said narrowing her eyes, as if she were a cat squaring up for a fight. 'Do you think we'd be here, enjoying the lifestyle our families have afforded us if "they" didn't care? It's called sacrifice. And I, like the rest of my family, will do it regardless of how we feel. And if you have any common sense you'll come into the fold as well.'

'I don't want to marry Hugo.'

'Then marry someone else,' Imogen said as if it was as easy as picking out a new dress from a rack in

Harrods.

'That's just it. I don't want to marry a man full stop.'

'All I can say is that you're being very childish. Not to mention short-sighted.' Imogen was starting to sound like Adriana's mother which was a tad frightening given her mother had at least thirty years on Imogen.

Adriana tore off a handful of kitchen roll and roughly mopped up the coffee spillage. With her back still turned to Imogen she said, 'I wish I'd never said anything now.'

'Why, because I'm not telling you what you want to hear?' Imogen said, her voice was unrelenting. 'That you should throw your life away because someone gave you a good fuck? Addy, no one is telling you you can't have that on the side—'

'I don't want to be unfaithful,' Adriana said letting out a weary sigh. She had seen too many of her parents' friends go down that route and the reality of it wasn't pretty. Lies, hate and anger were not the sort of emotions she wanted in her life.

'Then don't be unfaithful. At least physically. Watch porn, dream up amazing lesbian fantasies, but whatever you do, don't throw your life away on a dream that will soon turn into a nightmare.'

Adriana dropped the sodden tissue into the bin before making herself another coffee.

Deep down she understood Imogen's reasoning but Adriana's heart, the muscle that jumped with joy whenever she thought about Jessica, was in revolt. It begged her not to listen to a woman whose heart had never felt the joy of love. If Imogen had, she would have *known* that once love had you in its vice, it was too powerful to ignore.

'I know you probably think I'm terrible—'

Adriana drew up a chair and joined Imogen at the table. She didn't call Imogen over to argue. She had called her to talk. And that's exactly what they were doing.

'Don't be silly. I know you're just looking out for me,' Adriana said, giving her a reassuring smile. 'But what you're saying, it just doesn't sit right with me. There has to be more to life than just marriage, money and children.'

Imogen looked aghast. 'What else is there? What do you want to do? Live on a council estate shagging this woman senseless every day? How long do you think that'll last until you get bored stiff? And then what, on to the next one? When does it stop? When you reach sixty and realise you've made a mistake? A time when you should be enjoying your grandchildren, you'll be alone, too old to catch the eye of anyone.'

'What you've just described is my idea of hell. That my life at sixty will be all about grandchildren. Jesus Christ, at sixty I want to be still travelling the world, doing new things, meeting new people. This isn't about sex. This is about following my heart—'

'I can see there's no point talking to you. You won't listen, so I suppose you'll just have to find out for yourself.'

'Is that what you're going to do Imogen? Give up your only life because it's what your parents want?'

Adriana saw Imogen's eyes fill with tears and Adriana leant forward to comfort her, only for Imogen to hold up her hand. Adriana froze. 'I let go of the only woman I've ever loved, so yes, Addy, I'm going to conform and my children will as well—'

'If that's the case, you'd be better off not having any,' Adriana said suddenly losing her cool at the ludicrousness of it all. More than anything, she couldn't believe that Imogen, a woman who she thought was as forward thinking as herself, was trotting out this half-baked 'generational' philosophy bullshit.

And not only that, she wanted to put some poor innocent soul that hadn't yet been born through the same shit. 'That's just plain cruel, to bring an innocent child into the world and dump them in the same situation.'

The temperature in the room dropped and the tension was so thick it was suffocating. This was the first time Adriana and Imogen had ever had such opposing views and if Adriana was to be honest, she couldn't understand what had made Imogen so set in her ways. So compliant.

'Seems we'll just have to agree to disagree. I'd better shoot off. What's the name of the estate agent who's selling Beatrice's apartment?'

'Are you sure you still want to do it?'

'Yes, Addy, because I can. Do you see the benefits of the sacrifices our families have made for us?'

'It doesn't make it right. Or fair.' Adriana had to wonder if her own parents had married out of necessity or because they genuinely loved one another. What about her grandparents? No, she concluded they all had to have been in love. They couldn't have faked the affection they seemed to share. Or could they?

'The estate agent is Mitcham's. The one on High Street Kensington.'

'Shall I go for the full asking price or haggle a bit?' There was warmth in her voice now.

'I know you like a bit of a haggle, so go for it.'

'Fantastic. Righty, I'll let you know when I've done it.' She gave Adriana a tight hug. 'I hope we can disagree without falling out.'

'You're my best friend and I love you.'

'I love you too.' Imogen drew back. 'All I'm asking is for you to think about things before you go rushing in head on.'

'It's been duly noted.'

'Good!' Imogen wrapped her long scarf several times around her neck. 'Drinks tonight?'

'Most definitely.'

'See you at Raffles around six?'

'I'll be there.'

Adriana remained in the kitchen long after Imogen left. Her mind went over their conversation. Could she do it? Have Hugo share her bed, her life, her secrets and dreams? Would it really be that bad? Especially if she did what Imogen had suggested and have a fling or two on the side.

She glanced down at her phone for what seemed like the fiftieth time, only this time almost instantaneously a message popped up. At long last, Jessica had replied. It wasn't anything too telling. Just a simple question:

Why?

Because I miss you like crazy. Because I'm sorry I treated you the way I did. Because I want you with me always.

Instead of spilling her heart out in her reply Adriana typed back: **I need to talk to you about something. Can we meet up?**

Jessica: **I'll be home all day.**

Adriana**: Be there soon.**

***

All thoughts of why Adriana shouldn't see Jessica were soon replaced with all the reasons she had to see her again. Walking up the stairs, Jessica's apartment block didn't seem as grim as it had been the first time she visited, which she could only put down to desensitisation. Or maybe it was because today she was wearing rose tinted glasses and everything around her looked bright and breezy. Except Jessica when she opened her door. If Adriana had been expecting Jessica to look happy to see her, she couldn't have been more wrong. If anything, she looked majorly pissed off.

Adriana took a deep breath. *Keep calm,* she told herself. Jessica had every reason in the world to be angry with her after the way Adriana had treated her. But she had to get inside if she was going to try and make amends.

'Are you going to let me in?' Adriana asked when Jessica made no attempt to widen the door for her to enter.

Jessica hugged her arms close. 'Depends why you're here.'

'Why do you think I'm here?'

'What am I now? A mind reader? Just tell me what you want, Adriana, I'm busy.' Her tone was dismissive. A tone Adriana had never heard Jessica use before. Especially with her.

'I need to tell you something,' Adriana blurted out. It was the first thing that sprang to mind. 'Are you going to let me in or not?'

'Do I have a choice?' Jessica took a step back and gestured for Adriana to enter. 'You're going to have to talk while I pack.'

'You going somewhere?' Adriana followed Jessica into her room and perched on the side of the sofa. Even though most of Jessica's stuff was in boxes which were neatly lined up against the wall, the room looked smaller than she remembered.

'So you're moving, huh? You found somewhere?'

'Seems that way, doesn't it?' Jessica said, wrapping a vase with bubble wrap and placing it in a box.

'So where's your new flat?'

'Round the corner. The place came on the market yesterday. It's a two bed.'

Both sets of eyes fell on the bed and Adriana

quickly averted her gaze to look around the shabby room. 'I'm pleased for you. You deserve better than this.'

'In what respect?' Jessica tossed the roll of bubble wrap she was holding in her hand on the worktop, before turning around to face Adriana. 'You talking about this shit hole? Or I deserve better than someone toying with my feelings?'

Adriana rose to her feet. 'Hey, hold on a second. You think I was toying with you?'

'Are you saying that you weren't?' Jessica asked, raw emotion etched on her face. 'You slept with me knowing you might be getting engaged—'

'Would it have made a difference if I'd have told you beforehand?'

'What? Of course it would have. I thought you were single—'

'I was, I am,' Adriana said getting her words in a twist.

'No you're not! You're getting engaged—'

'I am not engaged.' Was Jessica right, in that she was 'technically' in a relationship even though she hadn't committed herself to it? Adriana didn't think so. 'I didn't come over here to discuss my personal life—'

'So why did you come?'

Good question. Why have I come? Before Adriana had a chance to think of a good excuse, her mouth opened and she found herself saying, 'Look, I know I could have told you this over the phone, but I just wanted to let you know that the money I said I'd give you when we find Edwina still stands.'

Jessica's jaw dropped and she stared back at Adriana with suspicion. 'Why would you do that?'

'Because I still need you to tell me when Edwina gets back.' Adriana let out a breath, relieved that she had managed to avert a major argument taking place. 'Or if you find out where she's staying for definite.'

Jessica smoothed back her hair. 'Really?'

'Yes really?'

'And what if she's in some far-flung country? You still gonna go out there to find her?'

'If you have the address, yes,' Adriana said, allowing the words to flow unfiltered from her mouth, knowing full well she would get on a plane with Jessica without a second thought, even if they didn't know where they were going.

'Okay, I'll keep you updated.' Jessica returned to packing the box with books and taping it shut.

'Do you need some help?' Adriana said, not wanting to leave but not knowing how to ask Jessica if she could stay.

'No it's all right,' Jessica said without turning to face Adriana. 'I think I can handle it.'

'Do you want to go for a ride in my car?' Adriana's voice held a trace of excitement that she hoped would entice Jessica to hang out with her.

'No thanks.'

Adriana let out a long, audible breath. 'How about something to eat?'

'Nope.'

Before she could stop herself, Adriana took four strides across the room and sneaked up behind Jessica, encircling her waist. 'How about we go to bed then?'

Jessica turned around in her arms, but didn't extricate herself. 'You think you can just waltz in here and expect me to jump into bed with you after the way you treated me?'

'I'm truly sorry. I was wrong to do that. It's just that I was scared—'

'Fine. Apology accepted. Let's move on.' Jessica's eager lips pressed against Adriana's before she even had a chance to finish her sentence.

Jessica's hands moved lightning fast over Adriana's body, peeling off her jumper, unclasping her bra strap, unbuttoning her jeans. Still stealing kisses, Jessica steered Adriana backwards until they reached the bed then gently tipped her over.

'I take it you missed me.' Adriana laughed as Jessica quickly undressed herself.

'Is it that obvious?'

Adriana tugged down her jeans and underwear and waited naked for Jessica to join her. The feel of Jessica's body was all Adriana wanted at that moment. This wasn't exactly how she had planned to spend the afternoon, but it wasn't the worst way she could think of. When Jessica climbed on top of her Adriana let out a long sigh. The familiarity of her body made her feel as if she had just come home. All the thoughts of what was and what had been between them quickly melted away when Jessica's hands slid between her thighs and she arched up to meet her.

'Feels like you're happy to see me as well.' Jessica grinned as her fingers slipped easily into Adriana's moist centre.

Adriana's mouth roamed over Jessica's neck, kissing and biting, then to her mouth where her tongue sought Jessica's. With each thrust of Jessica's fingers their kiss became deeper, slower. Adriana longed for the taste of her. With one swift move, she pushed Jessica onto her back and moved her mouth down her body, stopping between her legs.

The sensation that consumed Adriana was savage as the tip of her tongue slowly teased Jessica's swollen pleasure point, stopping now and again to savour it. When she did this, Jessica gripped Adriana's head with both hands, begging her not to stop.

Adriana kept her movement at a slow and steady pace, letting the excitement build in stages. Completely lost in her, Adriana continued until Jessica started to shudder under her touch. It was then that Adriana quickly moved on top of Jessica, using her pubic bone to grind against her centre, their bodies slippery with sweat as she increased the pace, until Jessica clung to her and with what felt like all of her strength, dug her nails into Adriana's back, bucking and writhing beneath her as she cried out Adriana's name until, with a shuddering sigh, her body went limp.

'Oh my God, that was so good,' Jessica said between short heavy breaths.

Adriana nuzzled her neck. 'You're like a drug.'

'Does that mean you're addicted to me?' Jessica said laughing.

'Hmm, maybe.'

Her laughter faded and she looked at Adriana with sorrow in her eyes. 'Are you addicted in the same way to Hugo?'

Adriana gave Jessica a light kiss on the lips before rolling onto her back. 'Do we have to talk about him?'

'Not if you don't want to.' Jessica trailed a fingertip over Adriana's erect nipples.

Adriana sighed in pleasure. 'I don't.'

'Then we won't.' Jessica snuggled up beside Adriana and wiggled her eyebrows. 'We'll just let our bodies do the talking.'

'Sounds perfect.'

Adriana hadn't expected Jessica to be ready again so soon, but Jessica was suddenly on top of Adriana, her hands urgent, seeking her out with a multitude of caresses. Adriana's response was to demand a release from the pressure building between her thighs. She held her tight, as she arched her back up so Jessica could press harder and faster against her until her world suddenly exploded. Their bodies seemed to melt into one another's as Adriana shuddered and her body became weak and defenceless. Adriana remained holding Jessica tight against her until the intensity passed.

'That bit of exercise means I don't have to go to the gym today,' Jessica said, drawing back slightly. 'Do you want something to drink?'

Adriana pulled her back down. 'No, I just want you to stay where you are.'

'I'm not going anywhere.' Jessica's voice sounded muffled against Adriana's neck.

'I wish I didn't have to,' Adriana said, closing her eyes. She was tempted to text Imogen and call off their date but after the way they had parted earlier, Adriana didn't think that would be too wise. Although Adriana wasn't in the wrong, thinking back over their conversation, she knew she could have dealt with the situation a little better.

'Have you got plans for tonight then?'

Adriana could hear the bewilderment in Jessica's voice. 'Yes. I'm meeting a friend for drinks.'

'A friend?' Jessica looked at her enquiringly.

'Yes a friend,' Adriana said, quickly adding. 'A female friend.'

'So this was just a brief visit then?'

The hurt in Jessica's eyes was evident to see. 'If you're asking if I came here for sex, then the answer to that is no. I came to see you—'

'To talk about my nan, yeah I remember.'

'And to apologise to you for being such a bitch.'

'Now you've done both, and you're leaving … again.' The crimson tint in Jessica's cheeks spread slowly to the rest of her face as she climbed off the bed.

Adriana blanched, confused by how quickly the mood between them had soured. Adriana pulled the sheet up to cover her nakedness, suddenly feeling exposed. 'What's all this about?'

Jessica looked down at her with narrowed eyes before her head momentarily disappeared as she pulled her t-shirt on. 'Nothing and everything.'

'Care to explain?'

'Look, I get that "this" isn't going anywhere, but that doesn't make things easier for me. Especially when we do things like ....' Jessica jerked her head towards the bed and the crumpled bedding. 'What we just did.'

Adriana sighed. Maybe Jessica was right. She was treating her like a toy. Mindlessly picking her up one minute then abandoning her the next. With this in mind, Adriana made a snap decision, and to hell with Imogen if she didn't like it.

'You could always come with me.'

Jessica gave a quick mirthless laugh. 'Are you serious? You wanna go out with me?'

'Why not? Unless you don't want to.'

A serene expression touched Jessica's features making her look quite vulnerable. 'Of course I want to. Where are we going?'

'Raffles. Do you know it?' Adriana wondered what Imogen's reaction was going to be when she rolled up with Jessica at her side. Would she be polite regardless of her own personal views, or would she be rude and sullen making the evening an unbearable one? Adriana hoped she could count on Imogen's good breeding to keep her thoughts to herself. She would text her and give her the heads up as she didn't want it to come as a total shock.

'Everyone's heard of Raffles. It's where all the well

off lesbians hang out,' Jessica said.

Adriana could have sworn she heard a trace of bitterness in her voice.

As if realising she had let her anger show, Jessica said, 'Sorry, no offence, it's just that my friends have tried to get in there before and were told in no uncertain terms they were not the kind of clientele the bar catered for.'

'It's all right. No offence taken.' Adriana knew of Raffles' strict door policy. Imogen knew the owner, Elisa, and had told Adriana that Elisa had instructed security on the door to keep certain types out. It was for this reason Adriana barely went to Raffles unless she was meeting Imogen. And Imogen only went there because it was the only place she knew she wouldn't bump into the woman she had an affair with.

'So do you reckon we've got time to have fun in the shower?' Jessica said playfully as she extended her hand to Adriana.

Adriana couldn't help but smile. 'You're insatiable, aren't you.'

'Only when it comes to you.' Her playful tone turned serious. 'Besides who knows how long I'll have you for.'

Adriana's heart sunk because if it was up to her parents, her gut instinct told her it wouldn't be that long at all.

Chapter Eighteen

Being somewhere that was normally out of bounds to someone 'like her' gave Jessica a mixture of pleasure and disgust. Pleasure that she had got past the gate keepers undetected and disgust that she took pleasure at being disgusted.

Adriana had popped to the toilet and left Jessica sitting at a table sipping a large glass of very expensive dry white wine. Not being one to deny being impressed when she was, Jessica gave the interior of the bar a massive thumbs up. It was thoughtfully decorated to the point everything had that extra touch. From the dim lighting, to the colour of the walls painted in a soothing willow that made you feel in a permanent state of ease. All the chairs were the same colour, a dark grey and the padding was so soft on her arse she had to wonder why all establishments didn't use it. The few times she'd sat on a chair in a bar for more than fifteen minutes, the pain in her tailbone had been so bad she'd been forced to remain standing for the rest of the night.

Jessica caught sight of Adriana walking towards the table, and could sense she was nervous about something by the way her eyes darted around the room. Had she seen an ex-lover? Or had one of the security guards somehow sensed Jessica wasn't one of the 'elite ladies'.

Whatever the reason, Adriana looked on high alert.

'Is something wrong?' Jessica asked Adriana when

she joined her at the table.

'No,' Adriana said, glancing towards the entrance.

'Is it your friend you're worried about?'

Adriana looked at her now and there was something in her eyes that told Jessica it certainly was this 'friend' that Adriana had concerns about. Had she been right? That Adriana was meeting up with her ex? After all, it wasn't unheard of that lesbians remained best friends with their exes long after the love had gone.

Adriana glanced down at her watch. 'Yes, she should have been here by now.'

'Relax,' Jessica said, resting her hand on Adriana's forearm. She quickly withdrew it when she felt Adriana tense. That was definitely not a good sign. Before she could say anything, Adriana was on her feet smiling at a woman heading directly towards them.

'Imogen.' Adriana engulfed her in a brief hug and Jessica could have sworn she heard Adriana mutter a warning of some sort in her ear.

'Sorry I'm late, bloody London cabbie. So what are we drinking?' Imogen cast a disapproving glance over at Jessica then totally ignored her.

'Wine?' Jessica said holding up the bottle in front of her. Maybe she hadn't realised she was with Adriana.

'I need a glass of champagne. Be a darling and come with,' Imogen said to Adriana, once again ignoring Jessica.

Now Jessica was pissed off. Once was just about acceptable but twice that was just plain rude.

'Have—' Jessica started.

Adriana shot her a look that told her to remain quiet and Jessica automatically clamped her mouth shut.

'Imogen this is—' Adriana started.

'Come on, I don't want to be in a queue,' Imogen said pulling Adriana towards the bar.

Jessica knocked back the remaining wine in her glass and refilled it.

It's a good thing I'm a happy drunk otherwise I'd give that rude cow a piece of my mind.

When they returned from the bar, Jessica could tell Adriana had spoken to Imogen about her rudeness by the way Imogen begrudgingly said hello to her. If you could call it that. It was more like a grunt. But it was an acknowledgement that Jessica existed and she wasn't in fact invisible.

To her surprise, Adriana chose to sit next to Imogen on the opposite side of the table making Jessica feel like the odd one out. If Jessica hadn't felt so insecure in her environment she would have pulled Adriana aside and asked her why she was acting so weirdly. Why, when they'd been intimate less than an hour before, was she now treating her like a stranger. It hurt to be side-lined because she wasn't deemed good enough by Adriana's friend. Because that's what it all boiled down to. Jessica could see the judgment in Imogen's eyes, the rude cow didn't have to say a word.

'Are you all right?' Adriana suddenly asked Jessica.

'Why wouldn't she be?' Imogen cut in sarcastically. 'Look where she is.'

The hard look in Imogen's eyes coupled with her

callous words caused anger to puff through Jessica like hot steam. Her body and mind flipped into flight or fight mode, and Jessica chose to stay and fight. She might not have money or a high social status but the one thing she did have was self-respect and no one was going to take that away from her. No one.

'What's your problem?'

Imogen arched a perfectly formed eyebrow. 'Problem?'

'Yeah problem,' Jessica said. 'And please, you can save your feigned innocence. I'm not an idiot you know.'

Adriana stood, her voice curt. 'Jessica—'

'Hey guys,' an attractive blonde woman called out as she headed straight for their table. 'I see you've started without me.'

'Only just.' Imogen shot Jessica a victorious glance before turning to welcome the newcomer.

'Anne, darling, so glad you could make it.' Imogen made a big show of how happy she was to see her. 'Adriana was just talking about you today.'

'You were?' Anne said making eyes at Adriana that immediately told Jessica that there was a thing between them. It was obviously what Imogen wanted.

'Imogen—'

Imogen turned her head towards Adriana. 'Don't thank me, Addy, I know how much you wanted to catch up with Anne.'

Jessica watched the scene unfold in front of her. If this 'show' that Imogen had obviously orchestrated for

Jessica's benefit was for real, and Anne was Adriana's bit of fluff, she would be majorly pissed off as it would mean not only had Adriana not told her about Hugo, but there was another woman waiting in the wings as well.

But from what Jessica could see so far, Imogen's plan had seriously backfired. Adriana remained frozen on the spot looking bewildered. That was until Anne strode over to Adriana, slipped her arm around her waist and kissed her. On. The. Effing. Lips!

This is unbelievable. Jessica hastily brought her glass to her lips and gulped down a mouthful of wine, nearly choking in the process. She didn't know how much longer she could fight both her anger and her genuine dislike for Imogen without doing something she knew she would regret.

'Whoa!' Imogen laughed. 'The flame's still burning between you two then?'

Jessica bit her bottom lip. She mentally gave Adriana five seconds to push Anne away. To tell her to take a running jump. But to Jessica's surprise Adriana merely stood there with a smirk on her face.

A fucking smirk! How dare you? What the fuck!

Anger threatened to boil over as Jessica stood, grabbed her jacket hanging on the back of her seat and strode towards the exit. With every step, Jessica expected Adriana to call her name, or at the very least be behind her trying to explain what the hell this was all about. But to her dismay, none of this happened.

By the time Jessica reached the bus stop, she had

just about given up hope. It was then she heard the footsteps running up behind her. Then a hand lightly clamped her shoulder. Jessica spun around.

'What the? Ariel?'

Ariel raised her hands defensively. 'Whoa, easy. Didn't you hear me calling you? I just got off the bus. I'm on my way to work.'

'Oh shit, sorry, Ariel.' Jessica glanced over Ariel's shoulder. Still no sign of Adriana. She gritted her teeth. Earlier in the bar, when Jessica had told Imogen she wasn't an idiot, she had been wrong. So bloody wrong. To have been taken in by Adriana again only served to prove that.

'What's the matter?' Ariel said. 'You look like you want to kill someone.'

Jessica kicked a stone on the ground and muttered. 'I do, three people to be precise.'

'Damn. Three? In one day?' Ariel let out a long whistle. 'I take it that Adriana is one of them.'

'Yes.' Jessica's eyes narrowed. 'And some slag called Anne and her snooty friend Imogen. Seriously, I have never met anyone so rude in my …. Ariel, are you listening to me?'

Ariel's body was erect, her back as straight as a rod and the colour slowly drained from her face. Ariel's eyes stared back at Jessica as if she was looking straight through her.

'Ariel?' Jessica said in alarm. She placed both hands on Ariel's shoulders and gave her a slight shake. 'Talk to me!'

'Adriana's friend.' Ariel's voice trembled when she

finally spoke.

'The bitchy one? Yeah, what about her?'

Ariel's jaw dropped open and Jessica heard a slight gasp escape her lips. 'Imogen? Long dark hair slicked back? A small mole above her right lip, blue eyes—'

'And wears bright red lipstick,' Jessica added, eyeing her warily. Had Ariel seen Imogen enter the bar, is that how she could describe her with great accuracy? 'How do you know—'

'She's the woman I was seeing, Jessica.'

Jessica's eyes widened. She must have misheard her. 'Imogen is your secret ex? Jesus, Ariel, were you desperate or something? The woman is hideous.'

'Believe me she's not.' Ariel smiled dreamily. 'She's amazing.'

Jessica looked at her incredulously. 'Are we talking about the same woman?'

'If she was rude, you must have said something to upset her.'

'Oh, so you're a victim blamer now?' Jessica felt her anger rise in response to Ariel's unfounded accusation. 'I never did anything to that woman, except dare to drink in a bar she thinks people like me shouldn't be allowed in.'

'Of course I'm not blaming you,' Ariel said. 'I just can't believe she was rude to you. She's normally really nice.'

'Nice?' Jessica's voice was ice cold. 'This is the woman that dumped you by text on your birthday.'

Ariel rubbed the back of her neck. 'She had her

reasons.'

'Why are you still defending her after what she put you through?' Jessica said.

'Because she told me at the start nothing could come of it. It's pretty much the same script Adriana used, isn't it? The difference being that I believed Imogen.'

'I believe Adriana now, trust me. I'm never—'

The familiar roar from Adriana's Ferrari's engine silenced Jessica's words. She turned her head and looked straight into Adriana's eyes.

'Get in,' Adriana said. It wasn't a question; it was a command.

'You must be joking, after—'

'Please?'

'Go on,' Ariel said. 'I'm going to be late for work. I'll catch up with you later.'

Jessica embraced Ariel before getting in the car. When the car took off like a bat out of hell, Jessica gripped the door handle for dear life. 'Where're we going?'

'To my place.'

'What for?'

'To talk.'

Talk? What was left to say that hadn't already been said a hundred times.

They arrived at Adriana's apartment building after twenty minutes of the most awkward silence Jessica had ever found herself in. Even if she had wanted to say something, she wouldn't have known which tone to use.

Should she be angry, jealous, indifferent? Or just plain sad because that's how she really felt deep inside.

That was until she walked into Adriana's apartment. Jessica was overwhelmed by its classiness. Chandeliers, polished floors, floor to ceiling windows, glass tables and the space. *Oh my God. I could get lost in here.* Jessica had to wonder, looking around in awe, just how much Adriana was actually worth. Jessica knew she came from money but she hadn't been expecting such splendour. Such elegance. Standing in the living room alone, Jessica didn't know whether she should sit. She glanced over at a comfortable looking window seat overlooking a small park. *What a view.*

Adriana came into the room barefoot and without looking at Jessica dropped onto the leather sofa. Seeing Adriana in her natural environment, only served to make Jessica realise how out of place she looked in Adriana's world. How much she didn't belong.

And to think she gave up a night here to sleep at my place. Jessica stared at her. The silence moved from neutral to uncomfortable in a split second.

'Aren't you going to sit down?' Adriana said.

'I'm fine standing.' Jessica shifted her weight from one foot to the other. She knew full well that she wasn't going to be hanging around for much longer, so there was no need to make herself comfortable. 'Nice place you've got here. Must have cost a fortune.'

'Is that a problem?'

'It wasn't a criticism, just an observation.' Adriana had obviously picked up the annoyance in her tone and mistook it as a slight. 'Look, why did you even bring me here?'

'Why?' Adriana paused, as if deliberately choosing her next words with care. 'Back in the bar—'

'Where I was totally humiliated? Yeah, what about it?'

When Adriana ran her tongue over her lower lip, Jessica had to use every ounce of willpower to drag her eyes away from her mouth and the thoughts of the immense pleasure it had given her. With a shake of her head Jessica tried to clear her mind. *It was such a bad idea coming here.*

'My friend didn't mean to be rude—'

'Which "friend" are we talking about? The rude one you let treat me like shit, or the blonde bimbo who tried to force her tongue down your throat?'

'Anne—'

'Who is she anyway?' Jessica narrowed her eyes. 'Your bit on the side?'

'She means nothing to me.'

Jessica snorted in disbelief. 'That's not what it looked like from where I was standing. Seriously, Adriana, why do you keep dragging me back into your life when I'm not what you want?'

'How do you know what I want?'

'It's self-evident.' Jessica's gaze swept around the expanse of the room, as she rapidly blinked back the tears that threatened to fall. 'You want all of this.'

Adriana scrambled to her feet and scurried towards her. Gently cupping Jessica's face in her hands,

Adriana's eyes brimmed with tears.

'I want you.'

Adriana's words were spoken with so much conviction, Jessica truly wanted to believe her. But the reality of their situation rebelled against the notion that they could ever be together. Adriana had already proven how much she cared about what those close to her thought. And that was never going to change.

Adriana leant forward and gently kissed Jessica's falling tears, a flood of emotions washing over her as Adriana pulled her into a tight embrace.

'I can't do this anymore,' Jessica said, unwittingly giving Adriana an escape route.

Adriana's shoulders trembled as she smothered a sob. Not able to let her go just yet, Jessica remained holding her for a few more seconds, burying her face in Adriana's hair, inhaling her scent in the hope of storing it in her senses so Adriana would always be a part of her.

Knowing this was going to be the last time that she would touch her was more than Jessica could bare. But she knew she had to leave before she succumbed. She knew to do so was only prolonging the heartache for both of them.

Jessica centred herself with the words Adriana had spoken to her on the plane. *Reality's a harsh wake up call.*

Dropping her hands to her side, Jessica backed towards the door.

Adriana looked at her with red puffy, pleading eyes. 'Where are you going?'

'Home.' Jessica took one last look at the woman

who had consumed her heart. 'I'm tired of this merry-go-round, Adriana. I want off.'

Adriana's choice had been made and now so had Jessica's.

Chapter Nineteen

It was just Adriana's luck that the one evening she turned on the TV to use as a distraction, there wasn't anything worth watching. With nothing else to help ease her aching heart, Adriana had consumed a bottle of wine and was on the verge of opening another, when her phone rang. Not really in the mood to talk to anyone, she ignored it. The only person she wanted to call her was Jessica, but the chances of that happening were zero to none.

The memory of the previous night came swarming back. Not only had Adriana quietly stood by and let Imogen belittle Jessica, she had let Jessica leave without telling her how she truly felt about her. That she loved her. And the thought of losing her had made her realise that she had been a weak fool, willing to sacrifice true love for the approval of her parents.

Is it too late to tell her now? Would Jessica find it in her heart to forgive her and let her make amends? Adriana reached for her phone and stared down at it. Before she called Jessica, she needed to be sure that her courage wasn't the result of alcohol. Because once the decision was made, there would be no turning back. She had dangled the carrot in front of Jessica one too many times before.

Jessica. She was surprised by the swift emotion of love that came by just thinking her name. This alone told Adriana this was the right thing to do. And that the timing was just right.

Refusing to think of the consequences of her action, lest they put her off, Adriana called Jessica's number. Closing her eyes as she listened to the ringtone she wondered how she should begin the conversation. Should she tell Jessica how she felt straight away? No, Adriana wanted to do that face to face. For now, she would let her know that there would no longer be an engagement.

Crap. The call went straight through to voicemail. Adriana took a deep breath.

'Jessica, it's me. I'm just calling to tell you that I've been thinking about us, and I know now that marrying Hugo would be a massive mistake. I want us to be together ... look can you call me back. I really need to see you.'

Adriana ended the call. *There, I've done it!* Almost immediately her phone pinged with a message. It was from Jessica. Giddy with excitement, Adriana opened the message.

I'm at work.
I finish at 10.
Come over.
 Xx

So she doesn't hate me! The doorbell buzzed and Adriana left the kitchen to answer it. Squinting with one eye, she looked through the peep hole and smiled when she saw who her unexpected visitors were. It couldn't be a coincidence that they had turned up out of the blue, just after she had made her life changing decision. Now was as good a time as any to tell them about Jessica. She just hoped they would understand her choice and support her.

Taking a deep breath, Adriana stepped back and opened the door to let her parents enter. 'Mum, Dad, come in.'

'Busy?' Alice bustled past her, handing Adriana her jacket as she did so.

Adriana smiled sweetly at her. 'I'm never too busy for you two, you know that.'

'Why didn't you answer your phone? We didn't know whether you were home or not.' Colin chastised her as the three of them walked into her living room.

'My phone was in the bedroom. Drink?' After they heard her news, they were going to need one.

'Cognac,' Colin said, sinking onto the sofa next to Alice.

The hairs on Adriana's neck stood to attention. *That's not a good sign.* Her father wasn't much of a drinker unless he was particularly stressed about something. Then, and only then, did he drink cognac.

She hoped whatever was wrong was not going to thwart her plan to tell them about Jessica. Adriana left the room and returned with a bottle of cognac and two glasses. She noticed her parents had suddenly stopped talking in hushed voices when she entered.

'Okay, what's going on?' Adriana eyed them as she poured their drinks.

'Have you spoken to Hugo recently?' Colin sipped

his drink then scraped his hand wearily over his chin.

'Actually, I want to talk to you about him—'

'Have you spoken to him or not? It's a simple enough question.' There was a hint of desperation in Colin's voice.

For the first time, she looked at Colin properly and noticed the dark shadows under his eyes and the grey stubble on his chin. He looked exhausted. Instead of reacting with anger which would normally have been her first reaction, she said softly, 'No I haven't.'

Alice played with the cuff of her blouse, a habit of hers when she was nervous. 'You've got to, Adriana.'

'Are you going to tell me what's going on?' Adriana said, determined not to panic before she had all the facts.

'We're in trouble.' Colin took a mouthful of his drink, causing his Adam's apple to bob up and down.

'What kind of trouble?'

When Colin looked up at her, his eyes revealed inner torture. 'The taxman kind of trouble.'

'You owe the taxman money?'

Alice and Colin exchanged a glance. It was Alice who spoke first, 'The company does. A lot.'

'When you say a lot, how much are we talking? Hundreds? Thousands, Hundreds of thousands? —'

'Millions,' Colin admitted begrudgingly, bowing his head like a naughty school boy.

Adriana narrowed her gaze and said with genuine concern. 'Millions!? Are you having me on?'

'I wish we were,' Colin said.

'But how?' Adriana now sounded like the parent not the child.

'Bad investments.' Colin grabbed the bottle by the neck and poured himself a large measure, which he knocked back in one gulp. 'We bought into a scheme that guaranteed to lower our tax liabilities, but the HMRC have decided it was a tax avoidance scheme.'

'Jesus Christ!' Adriana turned her attention to Alice. 'I thought you would have more sense than that Mum.'

Alice's eyes widened and she shot Colin an accusing look. 'This is nothing to do with me. It's all his handy work.'

'Dad, I can't believe it! You're the most frugal person I know. The safest. Why—'

'Why does anyone do anything? I got greedy,' Colin said, as if that would explain everything. 'It happens. I'm only human.'

Adriana shook her head causing her hair to swish with the force of the movement. 'I don't believe this. So when you say millions, how much are we talking? Two?'

Alice and Colin shook their heads in unison.

Adriana cocked her head. 'Three?'

'Six,' Colin said so softly that Adriana thought she had misheard him. But when she saw the shame in his eyes she knew she'd heard right.

'What! How on earth can you owe six million pounds?'

Colin jumped to his feet and paced the room as if he was in desperate need of burning off nervous energy.

'This is over several years. The problem is I've made bad investments since and have lost a lot of money. The company just doesn't have the cash to pay the tax bill and neither do we.'

Adriana's gaze followed Colin's every move. 'This is unbelievable.'

Alice cleared her throat. 'That's why we ... why we ....'

Colin stopped pacing and looked directly at Adriana. It was the first time she had seen her father cry. Colin's voice broke when he spoke. 'Why we need your engagement to Hugo to take place as a matter of urgency.'

Adriana frowned, not immediately connecting the dots. 'Hugo? What does he have to do with this?'

'His father is a very powerful man,' Colin said, trying to regain his composure.

'Very powerful,' Alice repeated nodding her head.

'If ... once we become family, Bob will refer investors to us. Big investors with deep pockets. I have a new cast-iron investment opportunity. This is the only way we'll be able to sort this mess out before we both end up in prison.'

Alice stood and went to Colin's side, giving his shoulder a reassuring squeeze. 'That's why we put Granny's apartment on the market so quickly—'

'Wait!' Adriana said. 'You mean it was you that wanted to sell it?'

Alice's cheeks flushed. 'I had no choice. We have to appease the taxman somehow, but once we've split half with Blossom and paid inheritance tax, what's left will barely put a dent in our bill.'

Adriana dropped onto the sofa and held her head in her hands. 'Why didn't you tell me?'

'Because we didn't want to worry you. We thought we could sort it out ourselves,' Colin said. 'But things are desperate now.'

'So are you going to help us?' Impatience sparked in Alice's voice.

The vision of a happily ever after with Jessica slowly faded from her mind. 'Do I have a choice?'

Adriana knew how hard it must have been for her parents to have swallowed their pride and ask for her help, but that didn't mean she didn't resent them for wrecking her plan to start a new life with Jessica.

'That's for you to decide,' Colin said, his voice breaking again.

Adriana pushed herself to her feet and went to her dad, hugging him briefly. When she spoke, she tried her hardest not to cry. 'Suppose I'd better call Hugo.'

'Thank you,' Alice whispered. 'Hugo is a good man; he'll do everything in his power to make you happy. I'm sure of that.'

That may well be. But he'll never make me love him.

***

It was ten o'clock and Adriana should have been in Jessica's arms making plans for their future. Instead, she was sat in her car outside Jessica's flat trying to find the nerve to go upstairs and tell her the dream she had of them being together had been wishful thinking.

Their new beginning was now going to be their goodbye. For good. Because once Hugo slipped an engagement ring on her finger, Adriana was going to be all in. For better or for worse. There would be no affairs, no secret dalliances with women on the side. It was going to be all or nothing.

She could have done this the coward's way by sending Jessica a text to say things between them wouldn't work out. But Jessica deserved better. Much better.

Adriana closed her eyes and drew in a shaky breath. They had been so close. And as much as she wanted to believe they were meant to be together, she accepted the possibility that maybe they weren't. That life had other plans for her. Like saving her parents from public humiliation and disgrace. If the investors found out that the company had been landed with a massive tax bill, the business would collapse and all of her grandfather's hard work would have been for nothing. Which is why Adriana had to do what was necessary. No matter how much it hurt her.

Five minutes later, Adriana stood outside Jessica's front door, her hand poised ready to knock when she heard Jessica's voice echoing in the stairwell. The door to the landing opened and Jessica appeared, holding her phone to her ear.

Seeing Adriana, Jessica halted, said a few more

words into the mouthpiece, then replaced her phone in her pocket and hurried to her, arms open ready to engulf Adriana in an embrace.

'I wasn't sure if you were going to come or not, I thought you were going to blow me out,' Jessica said.

Adriana had never seen Jessica look so happy. Which made what she was going to have to tell her seem even that much crueller. 'Shall we go inside?'

'Eager, I like it.' Jessica pushed the door open and motioned for Adriana to enter first. 'I even splashed out on a bottle of bubbly, okay it's prosecco but it all tastes the same to me.'

Because Jessica hadn't stopped talking, Adriana assumed she hadn't realised how quiet she was.

'Jessica—'

Jessica dropped her keys on the worktop and opened the kitchen cupboard. 'Sorry, but do you mind drinking out of a mug? I've packed the glasses away. I couldn't believe it when I got your message. I listened to it eight times to make sure I heard right.'

Adriana caught her bottom lip between her teeth. 'Jessica, put the cups down. We need to talk.'

Jessica placed the mugs down gently on the worktop and Adriana caught the flicker of fear in her eyes. 'I'm not going to like this, am I?'

Adriana shook her head.

'Just say it. You're making me imagine all sorts of things by keeping quiet.'

'I'm going to marry Hugo.'

Jessica glared at her with burning reproachful eyes.

'But you said—'

'I know what I said.' Adriana caught Jessica by the wrist as she brushed past her, and spun her round. 'I have to do this Jessica—'

'Why the fuck are you messing with me?' Jessica's anger became a scalding fury. 'To torment me? Is that how you get your kicks?'

'I … I ….'

'You what, Adriana, care for me? Like fuck you do. Marry him, don't marry him, whatever you choose to do makes no difference to us. You don't owe me anything.'

I love you. 'Jessica, I want to be with you. More than anything. But my parents are in trouble.'

'What kind of trouble?' The anger in Jessica's eyes was quickly replaced with concern.

'Their company owes millions in unpaid taxes,' Adriana said, feeling a moment of embarrassment.

Jessica's anger returned tenfold. 'So they're prostituting you off to pay for their debt?'

'It's not like that. They will lose everything. Their home, reputation, the business my grandfather built.'

Jessica blew out a long breath, her anger seeming to deflate like a burst balloon. 'I haven't got the energy for all of this. I'm so done.'

'Please,' Adriana said, fighting back the tears. 'I need you to understand why I have to do this.'

'All right, I understand, satisfied?' Jessica said. Sarcasm dripped off every word.

Adriana's vision blurred and she sucked in a breath. 'I don't want our last time together to end like this.'

Jessica gave a wry smile. 'How did you think it was going to end?'

Adriana pulled Jessica towards her and slipped her arms around her waist. 'All I want is to spend one last night with you.'

Silence surrounded them and Adriana waited with bated breath to see if Jessica would grant her the one thing she wanted more than anything. Suddenly, Jessica took hold of Adriana's hand and led her over to the bed. Without speaking they undressed and slid under the covers. Jessica lay on her back, and Adriana snuggled against her, nestling her face in the crook of her neck.

Adriana wanted to try and forget this was going to be the last time they would be together but Jessica's heart wrenching sobs wouldn't let her.

Chapter Twenty

Real life was no fairy-tale. Jessica had come to realise this many years before, but when she met Adriana, she thought for just one brief moment that it actually could be. During those magical days abroad anything had seemed possible. And last night, when she had listened to Adriana's voicemail, she had let herself believe that her happily ever after was finally within reach. But she should have known better. That life was just waiting to knock her back once again. Adriana's path had been chosen and she was going to walk down it, not with Jessica but with a man that she didn't love.

There was no bitterness in her heart, only immense sadness.

Though Jessica and Adriana had been awake since 6am, they still remained in bed, silently embracing. It was an unspoken understanding that there were no more words to be said. No discussions to be had. It was over. This time for good. Suddenly Adriana sat up and buried her face in her hands. At first Jessica thought she was crying, but then Adriana said, almost emotionless, 'I'd better go.'

Jessica said nothing. She was close to tears and knew if she spoke, her voice would betray her. The last thing she wanted was to lay a guilt trip on Adriana, so she watched in silence as Adriana got out of bed and dressed as if it was just another day.

Slipping her arms into her jacket, Adriana looked

down at Jessica and hesitated for a moment. Whatever she seemed to be thinking passed and Adriana leant over and planted a tender but brief kiss on her lips. Then, without saying a word, she rose, turned and walked out, closing the front door behind her.

Jessica pulled the cover over her head and allowed the tears to flow freely. She had no regrets, well she did, but only along the lines of regretting she hadn't met Adriana under different circumstances. Where Adriana was just a regular woman, working a regular job, with normal parents who didn't give a toss who she had a relationship with or how much money they earned.

But alas, it wasn't meant to be and Jessica was just going to have to move on with her life now, pretty much the same way Adriana was going to have to.

After wallowing in self-pity, which lasted most of the morning, Jessica showered and dressed. She had a lot of packing to get on with, which was handy as it meant she could block Adriana out of her mind by thinking about other things. Lunchtime rolled around and Ariel made an appearance brandishing a large pepperoni pizza with triple cheese. It was just what Jessica needed. Junk food and a shoulder to cry on.

Jessica hadn't spoken to Ariel for a couple of days so she wasn't up to date with her latest drama with Adriana. Or the fact that Jessica had worked her first shift at the Sleazy Slum the night before. After much discussion, Jessica had persuaded Mickey to give her a job behind the bar. As tempting as it was to jump on stage when she saw the ten pound notes being slipped in the dancers' thongs, she knew it wasn't a job she could do. Besides, the tips she got behind the bar were pretty decent.

'So what happened with you and Adriana the other day?' Ariel asked, taking a slice of pizza out of the box.

'Not much. We went back to her place—'

'And?' Ariel said impatiently.

'And it was amazing—'

'Because?'

'Because it looked like a feature in one of those home design—'

Ariel looked baffled for a moment then playfully slapped Jessica's shoulder. 'I'm not talking about her apartment. I mean what happened, you know happened, happened?'

'Oh that.' Jessica closed her eyes as the memory resurfaced. It still felt so raw. She could feel the onslaught of tears and she angrily blinked them back. Was she ever going to stop crying just thinking of Adriana. 'We ended it. For good.'

'Oh shit. I'm so sorry.' Ariel reached out and held her hand. 'I did warn you. To these rich people, family loyalty is an unbreakable bond. Nothing can come between them.'

Jessica refrained from telling Ariel the real reason behind their parting. Adriana's parents' troubles were no one's business but their own. Anyway, it didn't matter what had caused the final blow to their 'relationship'. Adriana was marrying Hugo and that's all there was to it.

'You never did tell me what caused you and Imogen to break up?' Jessica said, diverting the conversation away from Adriana.

'She couldn't handle the thought of us being permanent,' Ariel said matter-of-factly. 'Though to be honest, I always got the feeling she felt a lot more for me than she let on.'

'What was the final nail in the coffin?'

'I stupidly told her I loved her.' Ariel exhaled a deep breath. 'And that was pretty much it.'

Jessica rolled her eyes. 'Hmm, that sounds familiar.'

Ariel burst out laughing. 'Please don't tell me you did the same with Adriana?'

Jessica shrugged. 'Guilty as charged. Come on, let's go shopping. We need to choose paint for our new home.'

'Yay, I'm so excited. Just imagine all the parties we can have. All those women.' Ariel began clearing the table then she paused. 'Imogen and Adriana are weird women, aren't they? I mean any normal person would be over the moon to be told they were loved.'

Jessica stifled a bitter laugh. It had nothing to do with Adriana being normal or not. Some people were just not meant to be together, she now realised.

It was as simple as that.

Chapter Twenty-One

'So have you decided?' Hugo put his hand on the small of Adriana's back and she willed herself not to tense up. It was hard getting used to him touching her. So far it had only been a quick peck on the cheek, or a squeeze of her shoulder. But she knew it was only a matter of time before he would want more and she just hoped that she would be able to go through with it.

'I can't decide,' Adriana said, eyeing the diamond rings on the tray placed in front of her.

'Take your time,' Hugo said. 'I want it to be perfect.'

Adriana forced a laugh. It was strange how different things were between them now. At one time they would have been in a fit of giggles at trying to do something as grown up as getting married, but not now. Hugo's expression was sombre. He was finally getting what he wanted. As were her parents, who would soon be able to settle their tax bill. Hugo's father had already set up a meeting to introduce them to new investors. The only person it seemed who wasn't getting what they wanted was Adriana. *And Jessica.* Just having Jessica's name slip into her mind caused her stomach to churn. Was it always going to be like this? Or would she wake up one day, think of Jessica and have no reaction whatsoever. She hoped not. The thought of going through life devoid of any emotion scared her senseless.

Finally coming to the conclusion that she couldn't care less what ring went on her finger, Adriana chose the least expensive one.

Hugo looked at her selection in bewilderment. 'Are you sure that's the one you want?'

'Positive. Why, don't you like it?'

'I'm not the one who's going to wear it,' Hugo said.

No, unfortunately I am.

Twenty minutes later they were sat opposite one another in a small bistro café drinking coffee. Hugo had just finished telling her about a multi-million pound merger he had just signed and how they could afford to live anywhere she wanted. It struck Adriana as odd that a normal bride-to-be would have been ecstatic at having that conversation with her fiancé, but Adriana couldn't ignore the sinking feeling in her stomach. How different it would have been if it were Jessica sat here with her talking about how they would spend the rest of their lives together.

'Is Imogen going to be your chief bridesmaid?' Hugo asked.

Imogen was the last person Adriana wanted to think about at the moment. She hadn't spoken to her since their night out at Raffles. Adriana didn't know who she was angrier at, Imogen for being so rude to Jessica, or herself for not putting a stop to it.

'I haven't thought that far ahead yet,' Adriana admitted.

'Well you'd better start soon. Once our mothers

get involved, we're going to be married in no time.'

Adriana dropped her gaze to her coffee lest Hugo see the sadness in her eyes. Adriana saw it every time she caught sight of her reflection in the mirror. The heartache and longing had caused her once vibrant eyes to lose their sparkle.

'Yes I suppose.'

'Well on the bright side, I've finally got a ring to put on your finger for tonight's engagement party,' Hugo said cheerfully. 'Mother would have been most upset if we hadn't found one.'

Adriana wasn't sure if it was wise to be questioning Hugo on such matters, but she needed to know it wasn't just her that was entering into this engagement with trepidation. 'Can I ask you something, Hugo?'

He slurped his coffee. 'Anything. You know that.'

'Are you ready for all of this?'

Hugo frowned. 'This?'

'Marriage, living together, having two mums,' Adriana said, trying to sound light hearted but she felt sick even at the thought of it.

A slight flicker of excitement in his eyes told her he was. 'Absolutely. Aren't you?'

'Of course I am.' A wave of depression swept over her. So it was just her then. 'Just checking we're both on the same page.'

Hugo leant forward. 'The truth is, I can't wait for us to start a family—'

'A family?' Adriana almost shrieked. She was still trying to get her head around getting married. But kids—that was another thing altogether.

Hugo looked at her as if she had two heads. 'You do want children, don't you?'

'Sure,' she said, imagining how cute Jessica's children would be. 'One day.'

Hugo laughed. 'My mother has an obsession with becoming a grandmother. She thinks we're going to give her one by Christmas.'

Adriana eyed him intently. For some reason, she thought it was most likely Hugo that was pressing for this. Not his mother, who she happened to know very well. Tula was anything but pushy. 'You know that isn't going to happen, right?'

Hugo smirked. 'Accidents happen.'

Not to me they don't? Adriana drank the last remains of her coffee, anxious to leave. The more they spoke about 'his' expectations, the more it became apparent that they both wanted different things from life. 'Right, I'd better head off to my parents' place and help get things ready for the party.'

'Need any help?' Hugo said.

'No, I have no doubt the house is looking perfect.' Adriana got to her feet. 'I'll see you tonight.'

Hugo looked up at her, his eyes shining brightly. 'I'm so happy you agreed to marry me.'

Adriana opened her mouth to repeat his sentiments but the words wouldn't come. What could she say? 'Me too' when it was a blatant lie? It had been hard enough telling Hugo she would marry him. Adriana smiled, bent over and kissed Hugo's cheek.

Even though they were only hours away from officially being engaged, that didn't mean they had to go through with the actual marriage. Hugo might actually get cold feet and call it off.

It's a long shot but a girl can dream.

***

The music from downstairs filtered up to Adriana's childhood bedroom, where she stood looking at herself in the full-length mirror. Tonight, she wore a chic black dress and high heels. Her diamond necklace finished the elegant look as did the diamond ring on her finger.

So this is it, time to say goodbye to the old me and say hello to the newly engaged one. Just thinking that one thought caused tears to well in her eyes, which she furiously blinked back as she didn't want to ruin her mascara.

Adriana couldn't believe she was actually going through with it. No matter how many times she told herself it was for the greater good, she knew if there was any other way of getting her parents out of their financial situation, she'd cancel her engagement to Hugo in a flash.

A gentle tap on the door preceded her mother's appearance. 'Everyone's waiting, darling.'

Adriana sighed, steeling herself against the rush of emotions that plagued her. In less than five minutes her life would be changed for ever. And what made it even worse was the fact that Adriana was going to have to pretend she was happy about the engagement. She was going to have to plaster on her best smile for the photographs, listen while everyone waxed lyrical about what a beautiful couple they made while her real soulmate was half way across London probably going through her own hell.

'I just need a few more minutes.'

Alice walked over to her and held her by the shoulders. 'You are so beautiful, Adriana. Look at you, my little baby girl all grown up.'

Adriana stared at Alice and before she could stop it, tears fell uncontrollably from her eyes.

Alice took her in her arms. 'Oh, Adriana, please don't cry.'

Adriana couldn't talk past the lump in her throat, so she just sobbed in Alice's arms until her tears were spent. 'I'll never love him, Mum.'

'Not yet, but you'll grow—'

'No I won't. Not now or ever.' Even if Adriana never got the chance to tell Jessica how she felt, she needed to say it out loud to someone. Even if that someone was her mum. 'Mum, I'm in love with someone else.'

'Who is he?'

'It's not a man. It's a woman.'

Adriana could tell by the look in Alice's eyes that she was shocked. That this was the last thing she expected to hear. But somehow, she quickly regained her composure. 'I see. And who—'

'Jessica.' She wiped away a solitary tear. 'Mum, I fell in love with her the first time I laid eyes on her.'

Alice released her and let out a soft sigh. Her eyes

filled with sorrow. 'Why didn't you tell me. Look at the situation we've put you in. We should have found another way.'

'There isn't one. I'm not telling you this to make you feel guilty. I'm just happy I've been lucky enough to know what true love feels like.'

And for that Adriana would always be grateful, because she knew, if she hadn't met Jessica she could have been walking down the aisle never knowing what it felt like to be complete in body, mind and soul.

Adriana's phone rang. Glancing over at it on the bed she made no move to answer it.

'Aren't you going to see who it is?' Alice said.

'No.' Adriana reached for her make-up bag. It was probably one of her friends calling from downstairs to find out what was taking so long. 'Let's just get this over and done with. I need to redo my make-up first.'

The phone stopped ringing, then immediately started up again.

Alice crossed the room and picked up the phone. She glanced down at the caller ID then handed the phone to Adriana with a teary smile. 'I think you'd better answer it.'

Adriana looked down at the caller ID. Jessica. She looked back to Alice. 'But—'

'Answer it,' Alice said, stroking Adriana's cheek. 'I'll wait outside.'

Adriana watched her mother leave the room then turned her attention back to her phone. With a trembling finger, she pressed the accept button.

'Adriana?'

Jessica's voice washed over her like a caress and Adriana closed her eyes and pressed the phone closer to her ear. Even though it had been weeks since she had last heard her voice, it felt like an eternity.

'Jessica,' Adriana said, suddenly wondering why Jessica would call out of the blue. 'Are you okay?'

'Yes, have I caught you at a bad time?'

Adriana caught sight of her tear-stained face in the mirror. But her eyes looked alive and they glistened with happiness. Just from hearing Jessica's voice. 'No, not at all.'

'Good.' Jessica's excitement was unmistakeable. 'I just spoke to my dad. I know where my nan is.'

'You do!?' Adriana raised her voice an octave, then remembering she had a houseful of guests, she lowered it again. 'Where?'

'Corfu. My dad got the name of the hotel from her.'

Even as Jessica spoke, Adriana was unclasping the necklace from her neck and the earrings from her ears. She then kicked off her high-heeled shoes. 'How long is she there for?'

'That's just it, only for two nights then she's off to Africa.'

'Africa?' Adriana gave a slight shake of her head. Who was this adventurous woman her grandmother had sent her in search of? 'Did your dad tell her we were looking for her?'

'No, they only spoke briefly, the reception was bad

so they could barely hear each other.'

Adriana glanced at the time—6pm. She knew she was crazy for even thinking this way, but the prospect of finally handing over the letter to Edwina would put her mind at ease, knowing Beatrice would then be able to rest in peace. Not only that, it would give her the opportunity to see Jessica again. She had missed her so much.

Adriana tapped her chin, thinking of how she could get out of attending her own engagement party. She could just tell the truth and say it was an emergency. But Hugo would want to know the ins and outs of the problem. Or she could just slip away. *But mum's outside.*

'Are you up for a trip to Corfu?' Adriana held her breath waiting for Jessica's reply. If she said yes, she would find a way out.

'Are you kidding?' Jessica said. 'My case is already packed.'

There were tears in Adriana's eyes again, only this time they were tears of joy. 'Give me an hour.'

'I'll be waiting,' Jessica said.

Adriana slipped out of her dress and found the clothes she wore earlier. Dressed, she mentally prepared the speech she was going to have to give to their guests. The door opened and Alice walked in.

'Mum—'

'I couldn't help but overhear. So Jessica's found her grandmother?'

Adriana nodded, surprised by the knowing smile on her face. Had she overheard the part where Adriana had said she would pick Jessica up? If she had, she seemed to be taking Adriana abandoning her party in her stride. 'Yes. She's staying in Corfu—'

Alice handed Adriana her boots. 'You're going to need these. But put them on outside. You sound like an elephant clonking about in them. I'll take everyone into the dining room, then you sneak down and leave by the back door.'

'Are you serious? What about Hugo and our guests?'

'I'll deal with them. You go and deliver that letter. I know it's what Granny would have wanted,' Alice said with intent.

'You mean that?'

'Yes I do.'

Adriana stepped forward and embraced her. 'I love you, Mum.'

'I love you too.' Alice laughed. 'Now go and find this woman before you lose her again.'

Adriana didn't know who Alice was referring to, Jessica or Edwina.

Chapter Twenty-Two

The flight to Corfu was over before Jessica even finished her second gin and tonic. And now they were settled in their room in Japes Hotel—a small, cosy pastel coloured boutique hotel overlooking the sea. As it was dark when they landed, Jessica hadn't seen much of Corfu during the half an hour journey to the hotel. The outside world around the taxi was pitch black. But Adriana had reassured her that there would be plenty of time for sightseeing after the letter had been delivered to her nan. Which was going to have to be the following day, as Edwina's hotel was on a small island that could only be reached by boat and they had missed the last one for that evening. But that didn't matter, another eight hours and their search would be over. And their future? As of yet their conversations had centred around neutral topics. It was as if neither of them wanted to rock the boat. That if they somehow avoided the white elephant in the room, they could pretend things were 'normal'. A couple of friends enjoying spending time together.

But the big rock on Adriana's finger was a glaring testament to the fact that she was taken now. And if Jessica was being totally honest, knowing this made things easy. There was no chance of them falling back into old ways. This last jaunt of theirs, where they would finally complete what they set out to do, would be the perfect goodbye.

Adriana sat outside on the small balcony drinking a glass of red wine, while Jessica remained in their room going through the many board games she had found in the cupboard.

'Fancy a game of chess?' Jessica called out to Adriana. It was the only game there that wasn't aimed at the under fives.

'Absolutely,' Adriana replied. 'As long as you don't mind losing that is.'

'Losing?' Jessica laughed as she walked out into the warm breeze and joined Adriana at the table. 'I'll have you know, I won four chess competitions at school.'

Jessica's heart swelled at the sight of Adriana. Her sun-kissed body was barely covered by a pair of white shorts and a vest that left a provocative amount of visible cleavage. The whisper of desire stirred between her legs. If ever there was a time that Jessica needed an ice-cold shower it was now.

Adriana stared back at her with passion-filled eyes, sending a tingle down her spine. 'Really?'

'Uh huh,' Jessica broke their stare. 'But I have to confess, I was six at the time.'

Adriana gave a hearty laugh that washed over Jessica like a soft mist. 'You had me worried for a minute.'

'You should be. I still remember all the moves.' Jessica forced her attention to remain on the board as she placed the pieces on the individual squares. 'Are you ready for a whipping?'

'In your dreams.' Adriana traced her moist bottom lip with the tip of her finger, as she looked thoughtfully at the board. Jessica's hypnotic gaze moved from Adriana's mouth down to the swell of her breasts and she immediately wished she hadn't. Two taut nipples teased her.

Adriana made her move on the board then raised her eyes to find Jessica watching her. Instead of looking uncomfortable under her close scrutiny, Adriana's smile contained a sensuous flame that nearly blew steam out of Jessica's ears. It was then she realised Adriana was getting pleasure from teasing her. Of sitting there being in control.

'Oh, you want to be like that, do you?' Jessica said, deciding to go one better. Lifting her arms in the air, she reached behind her and pulled her t-shirt over her head and tossed it aside, leaving her bare breasts exposed.

A soft gasp escaped Adriana's parted lips, her eyes widened slightly and lingered on Jessica's stomach, then her breasts, then slowly up to her face. Her voice was silky smooth, 'I've missed you.'

'Me too,' Jessica admitted. 'I think about you all the time.'

'What do you think about?' The seductiveness in Adriana's voice wasn't hard to miss.

'Your smile of course.' Jessica rolled her eyes before letting her gaze roam freely over every inch by tantalising inch of Adriana's exposed body; arms, chest, neck, jaw, mouth. Finally stopping at her eyes. 'You?'

'Everything.' Adriana leant forward slightly. 'Hearing you call my name when you come. Feeling how wet you are ….'

Jessica exhaled a slow groan, her body throbbing with an unmet need. 'Are you trying to kill me?'

'There's nothing wrong with fantasising, right?' Adriana murmured.

From the expression on Adriana's face, Jessica could tell she was fighting her inner demons and she was losing the battle. So Jessica decided to make things easier for her.

'No, there's nothing wrong with fantasising. I think I'm going to call it a night.' Jessica walked around the table and whispered into Adriana's ear. 'See you in my dreams.'

***

Going to sleep with Adriana nearby had not been easy. Nor had waking up the next morning catching sight of her breasts rising and falling as she slept. But that was nothing compared to sitting in the back of a sweltering hot taxi without air conditioning. Every time Adriana spoke to her, she saw a film of perspiration glisten on her forehead, and Jessica's stomach went into melt down. Trying to talk to her while remembering their sweaty bodies thrashing against one another in ecstasy was near enough impossible. The best thing to do,

Jessica decided, was not to look at Adriana at all and instead, keep her focus on the stunning scenery. Doing that seemed to work and by the time they were on the wooden boat crossing over to a tiny island, Jessica had fallen in love with the idyllic place. What wasn't there to love? The sun shone in the clear blue sky, the sea glistened and the birds chirped and the people were warm and welcoming.

'I'm looking forward to meeting Edwina at long last,' Adriana said as they disembarked the boat and made their way to the hotel.

'And I'm looking forward to finding out what's so important about that letter.'

A short time later they were finally stood outside Capella Guesthouse, where Edwina was staying. Having already knocked, they waited anxiously side by side.

The door slowly creaked open and a short elderly woman, dressed from head to toe in black, looked up at them.

'Hello,' Jessica said smiling. 'Can you help us?'

The woman tilted her head in confusion.

Oh great, she can't understand English. Jessica looked to Adriana for help.

'Show her the photograph,' Adriana said.

Jessica pulled up the picture of her nan on her phone and handed it to the woman. The moment she saw Edwina her brown eyes lit up with instant recognition. The woman's head bobbed up and down in excitement.

'She here?' Jessica said gesturing to the inside of

the guesthouse. 'Woman. Here?'

The woman shook her head. 'Ochi, ochi.'

Jessica looked at Adriana who said, 'She said no.'

'She has to be here.' Jessica pointed to Edwina's picture again and back at the guesthouse. 'Ochi?'

'Ochi,' The woman said.

'If she's not here, then where is she?' Suddenly Jessica found herself in the grip of panic. Had they just set off on another wild goose chase? She certainly hoped not because if she didn't find her nan this time, she was royally screwed. Jessica had given up her job at the Sleazy Slum, on the assumption she was going to be collecting a hundred grand.

'*Grand Union … Grand Union*!' the woman said.

The words were music to her ears. Jessica pointed at Edwina's picture again. 'Grand union, yes?'

The woman gave a toothless smile, clasping her hands together as if in prayer. 'Nai. Nai.'

'Gracias, gracias. Ciao, ciao.' For some reason, Jessica found herself repeatedly bowing as she backed away.

Once they were back on the boat, Jessica noticed Adriana laughing to herself. 'What's so funny?'

'You just said thank you in Spanish and finished off with a bit of Italian.'

'You're kidding?' Jessica joined in with her laughter. 'From now on you can do the talking.'

When they arrived at Grand Union, Jessica let Adriana lead the way up the hotel's steps to the main entrance. The air-conditioned reception they walked into was empty.

'Shall I call out?' Jessica said looking out of a window that overlooked the pool area where several people were reading in recliners.

'Relax. I'm sure someone will be back soon.'

Relax? How could she relax when they were this close to finding her nan? Pretty soon she was going to be rich. Okay, not rich by Adriana's standards but mega rich by her own.

Adriana took a seat and patted the empty space beside her.

'I really hope that elderly woman wasn't telling porkies,' Jessica said sitting down.

Adriana playfully nudged her with her shoulder. 'Why would she do that?'

'Some people have an odd sense of humour.'

'Let's wait for another ten minutes or so and if the receptionist doesn't come back by then, we'll walk through the gardens and see if there are any other staff members around.'

'Sounds like a plan,' Jessica said and took a cursive glance at her watch. It was 9:20 and she decided that they would start their search of the hotel at 9:30 sharp. The minutes ticked by

and when the receptionist was a no show at 9:30 Jessica got to her feet. 'Right let's—'

Just then a woman sailed into the room, her white flowing dress billowing behind her. At first Jessica thought she was a guest, until she saw her name tag: Lucy.

'Oh, hi, you speak English?'

Lucy smiled and replied in perfect English. 'Yes, are you checking in?'

'No, I'm looking for my nan, have you seen her?' Jessica showed Lucy the photograph of Edwina on her phone.

'Oh, Edwina?' Lucy said with a bright tone in her voice, 'Yes I saw her a few minutes ago!'

Jessica couldn't believe it. They'd finally found Edwina. They'd finally found her. She looked over at Adriana who mirrored her look of elation.

'What room is she in?' Jessica said, turning back to Lucy.

'She isn't in her room I'm afraid. She left—'

'Left!' Jessica looked back at Adriana and rolled her eyes heavenwards to indicate her own frustration. 'I swear that woman is going to be the death of me.'

'That's not a very nice thing to say about your nan,' a voice suddenly spoke up from behind her.

Recognising the voice, Jessica spun around and to her astonishment Edwina was standing there. She looked a picture of health.

'Nan! I can't believe we found you!' Jessica ran over to embrace Edwina.

Edwina hugged her back. 'What are you doing here? Did you actually get on a plane?'

Jessica drew back. 'I sure did. I've been to Australia and Fiji looking for you.'

Edwina's eyes widened. 'But why?'

'Hello, Edwina.' Adriana stood and walked over to

join them.

Edwina looked up at Adriana as if she'd seen a ghost and the colour drained from her face. Jessica had never seen Edwina look so shaken and for a moment thought she was going to faint.

'Bea ….' Edwina's voice trembled as her gaze remained fixed on Adriana.

'Beatrice was my grandmother.'

Edwina's lips were now as pale as her face. As she lowered her head, tears trekked down her lined cheeks. 'Was?'

'Yes, she passed away.'

Edwina stumbled and both Jessica and Adriana grabbed each of her arms just in time. They led her to a chair and helped her into it. 'Nan, are you all right?'

'I'm fine. It's a little too hot today.' Edwina looked up at Adriana again, her voice when she spoke was no more than a whisper. 'I don't understand why you're both here … together.'

'My grandmother wanted me to hand-deliver this letter to you,' Adriana said taking the letter from her pocket and handing it to her. 'It was her last wish.'

Edwina reached up and took the letter between trembling fingers. Looking down at the envelope, she stared at the writing for what seemed like an eternity before pressing it against her chest. Tears continued to flow. 'Bea, Bea, Bea,' she repeated over and over again, her voice growing weaker each time.

Without noticing, Lucy had left the room and was now back with a bottle of water. She handed it to Jessica and looked sympathetically at Edwina. 'Bad news?'

Tears stinging her own eyes, Jessica said, 'Yes. Very bad news.'

A group of tourists wandered in and Lucy pointed to a set of double doors. 'Please, take her into the bar. You will have more privacy there.'

'Nan, do you think you can move?' Guilt filled every part of Jessica. Why had they just sprung this on her without thinking? They should have prepared her, how she didn't know, but anything would have been better than doing it this way.

Edwina glanced up at her with a glazed look of despair. She suddenly seemed so frail. So lost and alone. And the fact that Jessica couldn't reach her to comfort her, made seeing her this way all the harder. Then seeing Jessica's tears, Edwina seemed to slowly regain her composure. She reached out and took hold of Jessica's hand and Jessica could feel her still trembling. 'Don't upset yourself, love. This has just come as a bit of a surprise. There's nothing to worry about.'

'Come on, let's get you into the other room,' Adriana said softly.

'Please don't cry, Jessica.' Edwina got unsteadily to her feet. 'Look, I'm all right.'

Jessica could see her nan was struggling and the stronger she tried to appear the more Jessica sobbed. 'I'm sorry, Nan.'

'Why don't you order us some drinks at the bar. I'll walk your grandmother in.' Adriana gave Jessica a reassuring smile.

Jessica swallowed hard and bit back the tears. 'Okay.'

Nearing the bar door, Jessica glanced behind her and saw Adriana take Edwina in her arms and gently rock her from side to side. It was such a touching moment it made Jessica cry even more. The barman eyed her quizzically when she neared, no doubt because of her puffy, red eyes. Keeping her gaze lowered she ordered four brandies. She knocked one back at the bar and took the others to a table where she waited for Adriana and her nan.

Minutes later, they walked in and Adriana guided Edwina to her own table. She said a few words to her and Edwina glanced up and gave a grateful smile. It wasn't until Edwina was alone that Jessica saw her shoulders shudder.

Jessica half stood, ready to go to her when Adriana caught her by the arm. 'She has to deal with this alone. She knows where you are if she needs you.'

All Jessica could do was let her own tears fall as she watched her nan sat all alone, reading a letter from a ghost from her past.

Chapter Twenty-Three

Edwina had always known this day would come to pass. But even so, it didn't make the gut wrenching pain hurt any less. Edwina had lost most of her family and friends and she had taken each death as part of the process of living. But Beatrice dying. It was more than her heart could bare. The letter felt like the weight of a brick in her hands. The paper the words were written on would have been one of the last things Bea would have touched. What had she been thinking when she penned the letter? A pain squeezed her heart as she tentatively opened the envelope and took the letter out. A ghost of a smile touched her lips when she caught a whiff of Bea's perfume. The one she had worn since they had met sixty years ago.

My dearest Eddy

If you're reading this letter it means my granddaughter, Adriana, has found you. Oh Eddy, how I wish it could have been me who was now standing by you after so many wasted years. But it has taken some earth-shattering news to make me realise my whole life has been a waste. Without love, life means nothing. But you knew that. The money I gave you could never make up for the years we lost.

I'm holding the picture of your granddaughter in my hand as I write. Jessica reminds me so very much of you. The spitting image.

Even her smile. And it set in my mind that maybe, just maybe our time in this lifetime together wasn't meant to be. But our granddaughters—if they could be given the chance they could have the life that was denied us. I am certain Adriana will contact Jessica in order to find you.

Are they there now? Can you see what I imagined they would be like together? When you look at them, do they remind you of us? Let them share the joy and happiness that was denied us.

I want to go to my maker knowing that two souls won't make the same mistake that we did. We can't have our time over again but Adriana and your granddaughter can.

For so many years I pretended I didn't need you but who was I fooling. No one but myself. You, Eddy were the one I dreamt of with my eyes wide open. Who my heart beat for, when my eyes were closed.

Every morning when I awoke, there was a hole in my puzzle and you were the missing piece.

I would give anything to hold you in my arms one last time, but as I face my final days I can only pray this will come true one day. I will be waiting for you my dear Eddy, and until then I will watch over you.

Until we meet again, my darling, my heart has and will always belong to you.

Bea

Edwina slowly folded the letter and put it back in

the envelope. Turning her head ever so slightly, she watched Jessica and Adriana sitting side by side at a table. Even though her eyesight wasn't what it once was, she knew love when she saw it.

Beatrice was right. She always had been. It was Edwina who was in the wrong all those years ago. She was the one who had thrown away the chance of happiness because she didn't think she was worthy of Bea's love.

Edwina opened her bag and took out the picture she always carried of the two of them. They were so young and in love. And now history was repeating itself with their granddaughters.

Fate had given them the opportunity to right the wrong of their grandmothers' mistakes.

Chapter Twenty-Four

Jessica was relieved to see the colour had returned to Edwina's cheeks when she joined them at the table. Whatever the letter had said seemed to have rejuvenated her.

Edwina lowered herself onto a seat and gently took hold of Adriana's hand. 'Thank you for bringing me your grandmother's letter. You'll never know how much it means to me.'

'I can only imagine. My grandmother went to great lengths to make sure I found you.'

'That doesn't surprise me,' Edwina said, her eyes full of nostalgia.

Adriana glanced over at Jessica briefly. 'I would never have found you if it wasn't for Jessica.'

Edwina smiled at Jessica. 'It looks like Adriana is a good influence on you. I can't believe she persuaded you to get on a plane.'

Jessica grinned. 'Let's just say, she has a way about her.'

'Being Beatrice's granddaughter, I'm sure she has,' Edwina said fondly.

'Nan, you gave us a bit of a scare back then. What happened? Why did seeing Adriana have such an effect on you?'

Edwina's cheeks flushed. 'It was pretty much the same effect Beatrice had on me when I first met her.' She patted her bag. 'I suppose you want to know what was in the letter.'

'No of course not?' Jessica feigned innocence. 'It's got nothing to do with us.'

'That's where you're wrong. It has everything to do with you. And you Adriana.' Edwina took a sip of her drink. She looked thoughtful for a moment then smiled. 'Bea and I used to be lovers.' Edwina paused as if waiting for their reaction and when she didn't get one she continued, 'This happened a long time ago when the world was a far less tolerant place and Bea and I were from two totally different worlds. I worked as Bea's maid. Without being too clichéd, we fell in love.'

Jessica's brain had stopped processing her nan's words at the 'lovers' part. Her nan was a lesbian. Beatrice was a lesbian. She briefly looked over at Adriana whose face was expressionless then turned her gaze to rest on her glass. Had Adriana not heard what her nan said? Or was she just as shocked as her? Then she felt Adriana's foot kick her under the table. Jessica's head shot up and she saw that Adriana was talking to her with her eyes. Urging her to respond to her nan's coming out confession.

'Wow, her maid,' was all Jessica could think to say, all the while wondering if her grandad knew about this. No, she thought. Her grandad was so straight-laced he probably didn't even know what a lesbian was.

Adriana gave a slight shake of her head at Jessica's dire response and stepped in for her. 'It must have been tough for you.'

'It was very tough. More so for Beatrice than me.

I was free to love who I wanted, but Bea, poor Bea.' Edwina shook her head sadly. 'Her parents, your great grandparents were adamant she married well. That she did the right thing for the family name. She was dead set against it. She wanted us to run away together. Go to America, the land of the free ....'

Jessica sat in a stunned silence as it started to sink in that history seemed to be repeating itself. The only difference being that it was 2017 and she wasn't Adriana's servant. She looked over at Adriana for a moment and longed to know what she was thinking. Did she see the similarities of what their grandmothers had experienced and what was happening between them now? That social pressures were keeping them apart. Could Adriana see the consequences of not following your heart? The pain and regret etched in Edwina's features as she relived her past was undeniable and Jessica reached over and held her hand while she continued with her story.

'But I couldn't let Bea run away. I couldn't live with knowing the woman I loved would be banished, so I convinced her to marry the beau her father had chosen.'

'But if she loved you, why did she agree?' Adriana said.

'Because,' Edwina hesitated. 'I'm not proud of this, but ... I told her I would move in with her as her maid so we could still be together.'

'Oh my God, Nan, you didn't!' Jessica blurted out. She looked over at Adriana again and mouthed. 'Don't be getting any ideas.'

'So she married your grandfather. Oh we tried to make it work for years but it was too hard, for both of us. And when Bea had children I knew it was time I had to move on with my own life.'

'Do you regret it, Nan? Encouraging her to get married?' Jessica said getting caught up in the sadness of their love story.

'Every day.'

'But it was your choice to accept the status quo,' Adriana said.

'Yes it was but it doesn't mean I made my choice from a place of weakness,' Edwina said sadly. 'I should have made it from the heart. When we're dead and gone all of this material stuff will still remain. The only thing that's with us up until our last breath and beyond, is the love we have known. True love.'

'Oh, Nan. That's so sad,' Jessica said, saddened by her loss and the fact that they never got to have their happily ever after.

'So what're the rest of your plans, now that you have found me and delivered the letter?' Edwina asked, breaking into Jessica's thoughts.

'I'd like to hang out here with you, if you don't mind.' There was so much that she didn't know about her nan and she was desperate to find out who the real Edwina was. 'As for Adriana, she has a wedding to plan for.'

Edwina looked down at Adriana's hand in surprise. 'You're engaged?'

Adriana exhaled a soft sigh. 'I don't know. I don't know what I'm doing anymore.'

A small smile played on Edwina's lips, as if to say, 'mission accomplished'.

Chapter Twenty-Five

Adriana had booked a flight back to London the same night they had found Edwina. Though Jessica had pleaded with her to stay, she couldn't. Her mind was all over the place. She couldn't think straight about anything. Especially Beatrice. It hurt Adriana to think of Beatrice spending her life being married to a man she didn't love. Couldn't love. *That could be me.*

The chilling thought had quickly brought her to her senses. The first thing Adriana had done on her arrival back to the UK was to go and see Hugo. It had been hard to break off their 'engagement' but it had also been liberating. Adriana stood tall when she told him why she couldn't marry him. And to his credit, Hugo took it in his stride and wished her well, which she thought was very decent of him. Adriana just hoped he would find a woman who would love him and give him the life he wanted.

The following morning, she had gone straight to the solicitor with the letter Edwina had willingly signed and the funds from her inheritance had been released. The money she had promised Jessica had been transferred to her bank account and she had received a gushing text from her saying she could now afford that life coach they'd spoken about. As Jessica was still in Corfu with Edwina they hadn't discussed the future.

Our future.

With the paperwork finished, Adriana outstretched

her hand to Mr Griffin and he returned a firm handshake. 'Thank you for your help in this matter,' she said.

'There's just one more thing,' Mr Griffin said, handing her an envelope. 'It's the last of your inheritance. Your grandmother asked me to withhold these details until you delivered the letter.'

'What is it?' Adriana frowned as she pulled back the flap.

Mr Griffin looked at her kindly. 'The deeds to the ski lodge in Switzerland.'

In all of the impending chaos after Beatrice's death, Adriana hadn't given the ski lodge a second thought.

'Adriana?' Mr Griffin said.

'Hmm,' she said distractedly as she scanned the deeds.

He cast his eyes downwards momentarily as he fussed with papers on his desk. 'I hope you don't think I'm talking out of turn here—'

'Of course not. I know you were a loyal friend to my grandmother.'

'Good. Well you see, before Beatrice died she was concerned that you would use your inheritance to purchase her apartment.'

A chill ran down Adriana's spine. How did Beatrice know her so well? It was comforting to think that Beatrice knew Adriana would keep the apartment in the family and her memories alive. At least that's what she thought until Mr Griffin shattered her illusion.

'That's why Beatrice wanted you to have the ski

lodge. She wanted you to live your dream. To move on and enjoy your life.'

The smile vanished from Adriana's face. 'My grandmother told you that?'

'Yes. And she said to tell you, now let me get this right.' He looked thoughtful. 'Even though you'll be surrounded by snow, always have flowers in the lodge. She said you'd know what she meant by that.'

Adriana smiled, imagining Beatrice looking down on her hoping that she had learnt the lesson from the journey that she had been sent on. That unlike herself and Edwina, she would pick the right heart.

Yes, she would. Adriana wouldn't make the same mistake as Beatrice, she would re-write history with a happy ending.

An hour later she was stood in her parents' kitchen, with Colin looking at her as if she had lost her mind. But Alice gave her an approving look.

'I won't allow it,' Colin said with indignation.

'You don't have a choice. I've already made arrangements for my inheritance to be transferred to your account. You can pay half the tax with that. And the sale of my apartment will cover the other half.'

'You're selling your apartment?' Colin asked, looking aggrieved. 'What will you do for money?'

'I don't need money.' Adriana patted her left breast. 'I have all I need right here.'

'And Hugo? Where does he fit in with your plans? Is he on-board with you?'

'I'm not marrying Hugo, Dad.'

'You're not?' Colin looked perplexed as he glanced from Adriana to Alice then back again. 'What are you two hiding from me?'

'Nothing. Not anymore. Dad, I'm in love with someone else.'

Colin opened his mouth to speak, but Adriana spoke over him. 'Don't bother asking who he is because—'

'Colin, Adriana's a lesbian,' Alice said matter-of-factly.

Colin looked at her dumbfounded. 'What? But how?'

'I don't have time to explain, Dad, but just know I've never been as happy as this in my entire life,' Adriana said backing towards the door. 'She's coming back today. I need to get things sorted before I meet her at the airport.'

'Who is this woman?' Colin said.

'Her name's Jessica,' Alice said smiling at Adriana with love and acceptance. 'And I can't wait to meet the woman who has stolen Adriana's heart.'

'You'll both meet her soon. I promise.'

Adriana made it to Heathrow Airport just in time to meet Jessica's flight. Spotting Jessica in the arrivals lounge, her heart swelled with love. Adriana waved her hand in the air until she caught Jessica's attention.

'What are you doing here?' Jessica said, coming to a standstill in front of Adriana. 'I thought you'd be in Switzerland by now planning your winter wedding.'

'That's exactly where I'm going. In fact, our flight

leaves in two hours.'

'Oh, I was joking.' Jessica's face fell. 'So this is another goodbye?'

'That depends on you.'

Jessica looked puzzled. 'On me?'

'Yes, on whether or not you don't mind living in a cold climate.'

'Cold climate?' Jessica looked doubtful but said, 'As long as there's central heating ... Even if there's not I love being freezing.'

'And you're not scared of heights?'

'Heights?' Jessica grimaced. 'I am but you know what they say. Feel the fear and do it anyway.'

'And you don't mind helping to build a business from scratch? It's going to be tough until we start making money.'

'I've got a hundred grand if that will help.'

'One last thing.' Adriana sucked in a breath. 'Are you ready to take a leap of faith with me?'

Jessica took the plane ticket Adriana held out to her. Tears welled in her eyes. 'As long as you're a hundred percent sure?'

'I'm sure if you are,' Adriana said.

Jessica cupped Adriana's face in the palms of her hands and kissed her. 'I don't think I've ever been as sure of anything in my entire life.'

'That makes two of us,' Adriana said as she looped her arm through Jessica's.

Arm in arm they walked towards the departures terminal; the gateway to their new life together.

Printed in Great Britain
by Amazon